(B) Ballantine 24014                                    95¢

All new adventures of the U.S.S. *Enterprise* and its crew . . .

# STAR TREK
## LOG ONE

### ALAN DEAN FOSTER

*(Adapted from the animated series created by Gene Roddenberry)*

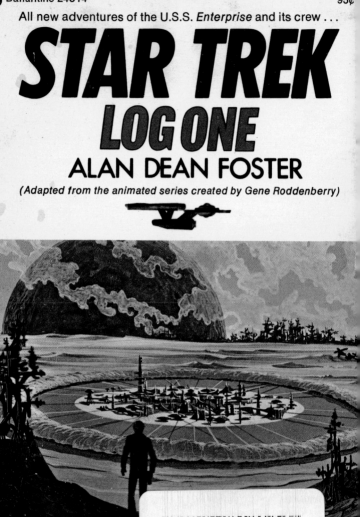

D0092838

# STAR TREK

*The show that would not die . . .*

Back in 1966 Gene Roddenberry convinced NBC-TV to give sophisticated science fiction a try, and *Star Trek* was launched. Getting the show on the air was a triumph in itself; keeping it on the air was something else again. Toward the end of the second season there were rumors of impending cancellation.

Viewers passionately devoted to the series deluged the network with letters of protest. Loyal fans picketed NBC's offices both in California and New York. The Save Star Trek Campaign—one of the most phenomenal expressions of viewer interest in the history of tv—worked.

So *Star Trek* was back on the air for a third season. Alas, however, many factors combined to lower the program's ratings, giving the network the ammunition it needed to cancel the series.

But still the fans wanted more . . .

Books about *Star Trek* were published, each one selling hundreds of thousands of copies to the faithful. *Star Trek* conventions all over the country attracted thousands of fans.

And now we have the exciting animated *Star Trek*. All the original actors are back aboard the starship *Enterprise*, assuring success.

Ballantine proudly launches the STAR TREK LOG series, publishing all the exciting new stories in paperback for the first time.

# STAR TREK LIVES!

## ABOUT THE AUTHOR

Alan Dean Foster was born in New York City in 1946; he currently resides in Los Angeles, where he teaches "Cinema" at Los Angeles City College. Upon graduating from UCLA in 1969 with a B.A. in Political Science and an M.F.A. in Cinema, he briefly worked in public relations. About that time, Foster began selling short stories to such magazines as *Analog, Galaxy, If, Adam,* and *Alfred Hitchcock's Mystery Magazine.* His first science-fiction novel, *The Tar-Aiym Krang,* was published by Ballantine in 1972. He quickly followed that success with *Bloodhype* and, most recently, *Icerigger*—all three novels set against the same fantastic background. Foster has also adapted the jungle movie *Luana* into a popular novel for Ballantine. He is now hard at work on *Star Trek Log Two,* continuing the adventures of the U.S.S. *Enterprise* and its crew.

# STAR TREK
## LOG ONE

Alan Dean Foster

Based on the Popular
Series Created by
**Gene Roddenberry**

BALLANTINE BOOKS • NEW YORK

For Judith
*Whom I Love*

SBN 345-24014-6-095

First Printing: June, 1974

Cover art supplied by Filmation Associates

Printed in the United States of America

BALLANTINE BOOKS
A Division of Random House, Inc.
201 East 50th Street, New York, N.Y. 10022

# CONTENTS

# STAR TREK LOG ONE

Log of the Starship *Enterprise*
Stardates 5321—5380 Inclusive

James T. Kirk, Capt., USSC, FS, ret.
Commanding

transcribed by
Alan Dean Foster

At the Galactic Historical Archives
on S. Monicus I
stardated 6110.5

For the Curator: JLR

PART I

# BEYOND
# THE
# FARTHEST STAR

(Adapted from a script by Samuel A. Peeples)

# I

Veil of stars.

Veil of crystal.

On the small viewscreen the image of the Milky Way glittered like powdered sugar fused to black velvet.

Here in the privacy of the captain's cabin on board the *Enterprise*, James T. Kirk had at fingertip's call all the computerized resources of an expanding, organized galactic Federation in taped and microfilmed form. Art, music, painting, sculpture, kinetology, science, history, philosophy—the memory banks of the great starship held enough material to satiate the mind of any civilized being. Satisfy and fulfill him whether in the mood for matters profound or trivial, fleeting or permanent, whether curious about the developments of yesterday or those as old as time itself.

Yet, now, in this particular off-hour, the man responsible for guiding the *Enterprise* safely through the multitude of known hazards and an infinitude of imagined ones that lay strewn throughout space—when he could have devoted his thoughts to little things of no importance and rested his mind—chose instead to study a smaller though no less awesome version of the same scene he was compelled to view so many times from the commander's chair on the bridge of the starship.

His eyes strayed idly to the lower corner of the screen. Gossamer thin threads of crimson and azure marked a spectacular nebula of recent origin—the flaming headstone marking the grave of some long vanished star, perhaps marking also a cemetery for a great, doomed civilization, caught helpless when its sun exploded.

Men in his position who would have deliberately chosen to observe such a sight fell into three categories. First were those for whom natural creation was too small. Men who found universes of greater magnitude within—artists, poets, landscapers and dreamers of hologram plays, sculptors in metal and stone and wood.

The second group would be that now dwindling but still sizable number of individuals who also looked inward—but whose gaze was forever out of focus—the catatonic, the insane, the mad . . .

The third and last asssemblage fell somewhere in between, not quite artists, not quite mad. These were the men and women who forsook the solidity of Earth, gave up the certain knowledge of a definite sky overhead and unarguable ground underfoot, to ply the emptiness between the stars. Starship personnel.

James T. Kirk was a captain among such, a leader of this kind—which made him, depending on which extreme you tended toward, either a frustrated artist or a well-composed madman.

He sighed and rolled over on the bed, temporarily trading the pocket-view of infinity for the cool, pale blue of the preformed cabin ceiling.

A visit to the Time Planet, where all the time lines of this galaxy converged—and who knew, perhaps those of others as well, for men knew nothing of other galaxies except what little they could see through their attenuated glass eyes—was their present assignment. A pity that time lines did not choose to make themselves visible to man's puny instruments of detection. Only one race had found that secret.

It hadn't saved them.

A visit to the Time Planet was always interesting. That wasn't its designated name, of course. But popular conceptions had a way of overwhelming scientific notation. He smiled slightly. There were enough new shocks, enough running discoveries taking place every time a new section of space was charted to cause the once unbeliev-

able Time Planet to recede into the land of the common-
place.

Kirk was a starship captain, not a historian. So his
prime interest in the Time Planet was from the standpoint
of its curious chemistry and even more curious physics.
The trip promised to be at least as interesting as previous
ones. But it was no longer possessed of that special thrill.

The remarkable view of the Milky Way in the tiny
screen was as complete a portrait of the galaxy as anyone
was ever likely to see. Few probes, even unmanned ones,
had flown further outside the galactic rim than the *Enterprise* was now speeding. Starships were too expensive to
operate and too scattered for Starfleet Command to waste
them on, say, just convoying experiments from world to
world.

That's why the *Enterprise* had swung wider than its
best course to the Time Planet, to enable it to take readings and star-map this section of the galaxy's fringe.

Kirk flipped a switch on the tiny console by the bed
and was rewarded with the view out the starboard side of
the ship—a view of almost unrelieved blackness. Here
and there were tiny dots of luminescence, dots which were
not individual stars, but rather distant galaxies—some
vaster, some more modest than our own.

Thoughts uncommon to most men raced through the
deepest pools of his mind as he contemplated that yawn-
ing, frightening intergalactic pit. Someday, he mused,
someday we'll have engines that won't burn out at warp-
maximum eight or nine. Someday we'll have engines capable of driving a ship at warp ninety, or even warp nine
hundred.

Someday.

Of course, the spatial engineers and physicists were
agreed that it was impossible for any form of matter to
travel faster than warp nine. Kirk thought that this belief
was simply a modern superstition. It had also been said
that man would never be able to fly or, wonder of wonders, exceed the speed of light.

An inship communicator buzzed insistently for attention. Again. Kirk looked at it irritably, then remembered
that he'd blocked off the channel. In effect, he'd hung out

a *Do Not Disturb* sign. He sat up and rubbed his eyes. There was nothing for it but to answer.

There were only two men on the starship who were on permanet, round-the-clock call. Doctor McCoy was one. He was the other. He opened the channel.

"Kirk here."

"Spock, Captain."

It was only a trick of aural mechanics, true, but somehow the monotone of his assistant commander seemed less distorted by intervening kilometers of solid-and-fluid-state circuitry than the voice of anyone else on board.

No, not completely monotone—for now he heard a definite hint of puzzlement in Spock's tone.

"Captain, I hate to bother you during your rest period, but we have encountered what appears to be a unique and extremely peculiar situation—"

That woke Kirk up. "An extremely peculiar situation" to Spock could be anything from just mildly serious at best to imminent disaster at worst.

"Be right up, Mr. Spock." He flipped the switch off, threw on his captain's tunic, dilated the door, and headed for the bridge double-quick.

Behind him, the miniature glowing panorama of the intergalactic gulf, forgotten, patiently awaited his return.

The elevator paused once, at B-deck, where Spock joined him. At the same time, the lights in the lift car and in the disappearing corridor beyond began to flicker. An all too familiar uneven yowling sounded.

"General Alarm." He looked at Spock, who replied to the unasked question.

"Lieutenant Commander Scott should be the officer of the deck, I believe."

"Why didn't he call me direct?"

"He did not say, Captain. But I think, if I interpret Mr. Scott's actions correctly, that he did not feel qualified to interrupt the Captain's rest period for a phenomenon of as yet undefinable proportions. He left that up to me."

Kirk considered that as the lift halted once more at the last level below the bridge. Dr. McCoy joined them.

"Jim . . . Spock . . . what's happening?"

"I don't know yet, Bones," Kirk said honestly. "You know as much as we do. Something that Scotty felt strongly enough about to sound the general alarm for."

Seconds later the doors split, and the three walked onto the bridge.

Helmsman Sulu was working busily at the navigation station. Uhura glanced back and forth between her communications console and Sulu. And from the engineering station, Scott looked up at their arrival and let out a visible sigh of relief.

"Glad to see you, Captain. I wasn't ready for makin' too many more decisions. Not considerin' the nature of this thing, whatever it is."

Spock went directly to his library computer seat—the control station for the brain and nervous system of the *Enterprise*. As Kirk took his own place in the command chair, he noted that the alarm system was still sounding its howling warning.

"That's enough noise, Mr. Sulu." Sulu nodded. Lights and alarm returned to normal status.

"Situation, Mr. Scott?"

Kirk was already studying the projected vector-grid Sulu had thrown up on the main screen. In a lower right-hand quadrant, the white dot of the *Enterprise* was moving rapidly centerward—too rapidly, Kirk thought.

He envied the old sea captains of Earth's ancient days, when a vessel's energy came only from the blowing winds, envied a skipper who could feel a change in his ship's speed through his feet. Out here in black, uncaring vacuum, there was nothing to push against, nothing to feel against you. Compared to a rambunctious sea or strong gale, artificial gravity was a poor stimulant.

Man's senses only operated here artificially, through enormous mechanical amplification—and the only waves one could get the feel of were in wave mechanics.

"We've picked up speed, sir," informed Scott, confirming Kirk's analysis of the situation depicted on the screen. "A great deal of speed!"

"Cut back, then, Scotty."

"I've already done so, sir—cut back twice—but we continue to gain momentum!"

"Now don't get excited, Mr. Scott—" The question had to be asked, despite any damage that might incur to the engineer's pride. "—but have you checked your instrumentation?"

"Aye, Captain, checked, and triple-checked. I'd prefer the instrumentation *were* off, than to have to proceed with these readings. No sir, the information is correct." He gestured in the direction of the vector-grid.

Kirk swiveled slightly in the chair. "Mr. Sulu?"

If anything, Sulu's expression was twice as worried and half again as uncertain as the chief engineer's.

"She's not answering the helm, sir! We're—" he paused to check his own readouts, "—two minutes right ascension off course." He hammered at the stubborn controls in front of him, as if that might have some naturalizing effect on the incredible information coming in.

"And drifting farther off every second, sir."

"Mr. Spock."

"Captain?"

"Do me an in-depth computer-library scan on all known major stellar bodies in this fringe sector."

"Yes, Captain."

"And put it up on the big screen when it's ready."

There was a brief, quiet pause. Nothing moved on the bridge except the white dot of the *Enterprise* on the viewscreen. Then the vector-grid was replaced by another, an overlay star-map. Or rather, part of the grid was replaced. Three-quarters of the screen did not light up with the light blue of completed mappings. It remained maddeningly blank—except for one large word in yellow, a word Kirk had almost expected to see.

UNEXPLORED

A second later, information appeared beneath this first disappointing word in the form of the legend.

*To Be Mapped—No Accurate Data Currently Available.*

"That's what I thought, Mr. Spock. But there was a chance. Information comes into Starfleet's banks so fast these days."

"Evidently not fast enough, Captain."

"No. Not fast enough. That'll do, Spock."

The uninformative star-map overlay blanked out and the vector-grid dominated the entire screen once more.

"Captain?" The call came from the rear of the bridge.

"Yes, Uhura?"

She seemed confused. "Captain, I've been picking up strong, but very strange radio emissions for the past two hours. Both source and direction were at first far to the right plane of our course. But since our position has been shifting, the source of emission and the course of the *Enterprise* are lining up."

Kirk considered this piece of news. It was not especially foreboding. Not yet, anyway.

"All right, Uhura, I'll keep it in mind." He looked back at the screen. "At least there's something out there."

The white pinpoint continued to move purposefully across the grid, drawn by ... what? He could reach out with a forefinger and blot the great starship from view. At the same time he reached a decision. While whatever was pulling them off course had shown nothing that could be definitely interpreted as a hostile action—it was probably a natural phenomenon anyway—it still behooved them to put up some form of resistance.

"Mr. Sulu, stand by to back engines."

"Standing by, sir." Sulu divided his attention between the screen and his bank of controls.

"Back engines."

The helmsman's hands moved over the navigation console, flipped a last knob 180 degrees. A slight jar traveled through the bridge, followed by a distant but distinct rumbling. Everyone made an instinctive grab for the nearest solid object. But only the slight jar gave evidence of the tremendous stresses operating on the starship.

Kirk stared at the vector-grid intently. The white dot slowed perceptibly, slowed ... but continued on its new path, moving inexorably forward.

"Mr. Spock," Kirk demanded, "have you got anything yet?" We'd operate a helluva lot more effectively if we had some idea of what we were up against, Kirk thought.

Spock had remained glued to the hooded viewer of the computer readout. Now he looked up and over at the captain's position.

"At this point, Captain, I can only say we are headed toward an unknown object—probably natural, probably of at least planetary mass—that is generating a remarkable amount of hyper-gravity. Hyper-gravity more concentrated than any we have ever encountered."

"Well, if there's something like that out there," and Kirk gestured at the screen, "that can put out that kind of pull plus radio emissions, why aren't our evaluative sensors picking it up?" He rolled his fingers against one leg. "Open the forward scanners all the way, Mr. Sulu, and close off everything else. Divert all sensor power forward."

"All of it, sir?"

"All of it."

There was a moment's rush of activity as Sulu hurried to comply with the order. It left them uncomfortably vulnerable to anything that might choose to sneak up on the ship from any direction but ahead. But what could be sneaking around, out here on the galaxy's rim?

The screen flickered. The vector-grid vanished. Extending from the left side of the screen two-thirds of the way across now was the outermost arm of the Milky Way. A distant, ethereal packing of rainbow-hued dust. The other third, except for a few scattered, lonely spots of brilliance, was black with the blackness of the intergalactic abyss.

But in the center of the screen . . .

In the center, something was taking a smooth, crescent-shaped bite out of the glowing star-mist that formed the arm. Something spherical, small—but growing. A globe of nothingness that was obscuring star after star.

No, not entirely nothing, now. As they moved nearer, a distant, faint glint gave evidence of a solid surface. Fascinated, Kirk and the rest of the bridge personnel stared at the unknown, dark wanderer. They tried to define, pin down, regularize its maddeningly elusive silhouette.

Uhura finally broke the silence.

"Captain, that's definitely the source of the emissions. They've changed considerably since I first detected them. And they've also grown much stronger since we've moved close."

"Pipe them over the communicators, Uhura. Don't keep it a secret."

She hit a single control. Immediately the bridge was filled with a shrill, piercing electronic hum. She smiled apologetically and reduced the deafening volume. As the sound became bearable one thing was instantly obvious to the lowliest ensign. That whine was too wild, too powerful to come from an artificial source. It was as natural an extrusion of the object ahead as a solar prominence or a man's arm. It was definitely *not* the product of a constructed beacon or station.

Everyone listened to the alien hum as the outline on the viewscreen continued to grow, eating away at the distant star-field.

"Mr. Scott, ready your engineers for a maximum effort."

"Aye, sir." Scott turned to his direct line back to engineering.

"Davis, Gradner, get off your duffs! The captain's going to be wantin' some work out 'o ye in a moment—"

"Mr. Sulu," Kirk continued, "stay on these back engines."

"Yes, sir."

"Mr. Spock," and Kirk tried not to sound desperate, "anything yet?"

"Sir, I've had the computers working since we first entered the peculiar gravity-well, but I hesitated to offer an opinion on preliminary sensor data alone. Now that we have achieved visual confirmation, I no longer hesitate."

Spock's eyebrows shot way up, which surprised Kirk. For Spock that was an expression of astonishment equivalent to an audible gasp from a human. Something unique was surely in the offing.

"It is a negative star-mass, Captain, Spectroanalysis confirms finally ninety-seven point eight percent probability that the object ahead of us is composed of imploded matter. Every reading on material composition records in the negative."

"Great! That means we're headed toward an immensely powerful aggregation of nothing?"

"That is rather more colloquial than I should put it, Captain, but it is effectively descriptive."

Sulu chose that moment to interrupt with additional happy news. "Captain, our speed is increasing again!"

That did it. "All engines, full reverse thrust!"

There was a long pause as another jar and a following rumble ran through the *Enterprise*. Then Sulu looked up from the helm. He didn't appear panicked—he was too good an officer for that—but he was clearly worried.

"It's no good, sir, we're still falling toward it."

"Mr. Scott," said Kirk tightly, "what's the matter with those engines of yours?"

"There's nothin' wrong with the engines, sir," the chief engineer replied evenly. "They're doin' their best, sir, but they're badly overmatched. They're designed to push ... not pull against a gravity-well as deep as this! I'm not sure we could pull free now if we had ten times the power."

Kirk looked back at the screen, where the negative stellar mass now all but filled the forward view, blotting out the last visible stars. With the decreased distance, more of the surface had become visible. Dull black in color, it was pockmarked with ancient craters—uneven and clearly, inarguably dead. Occasionally a startlingly bright bolt of electrical energy would arc between high points on the surface, leaping from crag to crag like a stone skipping over a pond.

To be visible at such a distance the bolts must have been enormous.

"How much time do we have?"

Spock replied easily, evenly, without looking away from his viewer. "Impact in ninety-three seconds, Captain. Ninety-two ... ninety-one ... "

Stunned silence suddenly filled the bridge. It had all happened so fast. One minute they were in minor difficulty, experiencing some strange, slight course deflection, and then—

No one saw the strange expression come over Uhura's face. She flicked a long nail against one earphone, then the other. No, the instruments were working properly, all right.

"Captain, I'm picking up a new signal. Listen." She moved delicate fingers over the console.

The drone of the dead star filled the bridge. But sounding over it now was a second, distinct whine, almost a wailing cry. More importantly, the sound was clearly modulated, obviously emanating from an artificial source. It faded in and out at lonely, regular intervals.

"Forty seconds, Captain," intoned Spock. For all the excitement he exhibited he might as well have been reciting the time left on a baking cake.

"Thirty-nine . . . thirty-eight . . ."

Inside, Kirk was fuming. Time, time . . . ! They couldn't go forward and they couldn't go back. That left . . .

"Mr. Sulu!" he barked abruptly. "Flank speed ahead! Declension thirty degrees."

"*Ahead*, sir?"

"MOVE IT, MR. SULU!" The helmsman moved. Maybe the hyper-gravity helped.

"We've got one chance at this point. That's to make a safe orbit. After that, we can figure out a way to break away at our leisure. I need more than thirty seconds for that."

Sulu moved rapidly at the controls. His body became a soft, fleshy extension of the *Enterprise*'s navigation system. Like Aladdin, he had only to present his wishes in comprehensible form and the electronic genie would handle the details.

But would it have enough ability to counter the titanic black demon sucking them forward to destruction?

Kirk stared at the screen, now wholly occupied by the shape of the dead star. If their bid for orbit failed, no one would ever know it. The death of the *Enterprise* wouldn't even be recorded by an idle astronomer on some distant planet as a tiny flash in far space. The massive gravity-well of the negative mass would swallow light as well as life.

"Nine seconds," came Spock's calm voice. Only a slight rise in pitch betrayed any hint of anxiety, excitement. "Eight. . . .seven. . . ."

It was absurd Kirk thought, holding tightly to the command chair! That wouldn't prolong his life by the minutest fraction of a second. But his hands continued to grip the unyielding metal nonetheless.

An electrical discharge thousands of kilometers in

length lit the screen for an instant, impossibly close. Then, it was gone—and so was the blackness. Ahead once again lay the friendly, fluorescing mists of the galaxy, and the honest darkness of open space.

But Kirk knew this vision of escape was illusory. A second later Sulu confirmed it.

"No breakaway, Captain, but insertion accomplished." He sighed in visible relief. "Details of orbit to follow. We'll have a low perigee, damn low, but—" he smiled, "not low enough to drop us out of orbit."

"Praise the Lord and pass the ammunition!" called Scott.

"I beg your pardon, Mr. Scott?"

"Nothin', Spock, nothin'."

"I beg your pardon again, Mr. Scott, but you definitely said something, not nothing." Scott gave him a pained look, and Spock suddenly comprehended.

"Ah, I see. The use of nonreferential archaic terminology served to audibilize the otherwise inexpressable emotions you felt at the moment."

"So would a punch in the snoot, pointy-ears!" warned the chief engineer.

"Is that a further audibilization?"

Kirk looked away so they wouldn't see the broad grin spreading across his face.

"Give up, Mr. Scott, you're fighting a losing battle."

"Aye, Captain," acknowledged Scott disgustedly. "I've an easier time communicatin' with a number-four automatic welder!" Then he too smiled, but only briefly. Current thoughts were too serious.

"Speakin' of which, Captain, if we don't need the power right now, it'd be a good thing for the engines to go on minimum, after all the time they spent puttin' out maximum reverse thrust."

"Yes, of course, Scotty. Mr. Sulu, compute the minimum drive we need to hold this orbit without falling and feed the data to Mr. Scott for issuance to engineering."

"Yes, sir." Moments later, "Ready, sir."

"Fine, Lieutenant. Now activate rear scanners and put our stern towards the mass."

There was a wait while the view in the big screen

seemed to rotate. Actually it was the ship that was changing position and not the universe. The star-field was gradually replaced by a fresh picture, a view of the ebony sphere turning slowly below them.

"Mr. Spock, final orbit confirmation?"

"We are holding this orbital configuration easily, Captain. Effectively standoff has been achieved."

"Good. Steady as she goes, then, Mr. Sulu."

"Aye, aye, sir." The lieutenant couldn't keep an admiring tone from creeping into his voice. Kirk glanced away, slightly embarrassed.

Dr. McCoy observed the captain's reaction and grinned. No one had noticed his arrival on the bridge. They had all been, to say the least, otherwise occupied. For his part, McCoy had kept quiet. He had had nothing to say that could have been of any help, and the situation when he had arrived called for anything but a dose of his dry wit.

Now, however, some idle conversation might have its therapeutic values. He had a degree in that, as well as in medicine.

"If its pull is so strong, Jim, how do we ever break out of its grip?"

"What? Oh, hello, Bones." Kirk turned his chair a little. "One thing at a time. If we'd known what we were heading for soon enough, I'd have at least tried a cometary orbit. But by the time we knew for sure what we were up against, it was too late." He looked over at the library console.

"But you're right—it's a question we'll have to deal with eventually. How about a slingshot effect, Mr. Spock? Have we got enough power to break out at the last second? We can run on maximum overdrive for the necessary time. We'll have to dive as close as possible to the surface before pulling out, to make maximum use of the gravity-well's catapulting power. If we don't make it, we'll end up so many odd-sized blobs on the surface. Don't forget, Bones, it's attractive force increases exponentially as we near the actual surface."

Spock didn't answer the opening query right away, instead stayed bent over the viewer and continued to work.

"I'll need some time for the computations to go through, Captain. Power, orbit, proper distance from the stellar surface, angle of descent, crucial altitude. Information is still coming in through our sensors at a tremendous rate. Our knowledge of hyper-gravity is woefully slim. This is the first time a starship has been so close to a negative stellar mass. At least, the first time one has been this close and survived.

"There are too many variables at this point for hasty calculation. I can't give you an answer yet."

"All right, Spock. Set the computer on the problem. We'll learn as we orbit. We've nothing else to do, anyway. Starfleet will go crazy over the data."

As if on cue, Uhura broke in. "Excuse me, Captain, but I'm picking up that secondary signal again. We lost it temporarily when we powered into orbit, but I've got it back." She paused. "Or else *it's* got *us* back. Nine seconds north inclination, dead ahead and closing fast."

"Is it . . . ?" he began, but Uhura guessed the question.

"No, Captain. We're coming up on it, not vice-versa. Still, I wonder."

"The universe is full of coincidences, Lieutenant. How soon till sensor contact?"

"It should be on the screens in a minute, Captain."

Everyone on the bridge turned full attention to the shifting view in the main screen. For long moments there was little change in the picture. Then a faintly luminous jumble of tiny lines appeared. It began to increase rapidly in size.

Even at this distance it was easy to see that the object was an artificial construct and not a natural body. But there must be something wrong with the sensors. It was too far away to appear so large.

"Can we slow enough to match orbits, Mr. Sulu, without dropping beyond the safe range?"

Sulu fumbled with the navigation computer. "Have the answer in a second, sir." He paused. "Yes sir, no difficulty, sir. We have a respectable margin."

"Then put us alongside as we come up on it."

The object grew speedily until it dominated the viewscreen as the dead sun had before. Sulu had to reduce perspective twice to keep the entire shape in full view. Suddenly there was silence on the bridge when it became apparent what the shape was.

## II

The starship was beautiful.

All the more so in contrast to the stark dead giant that held them trapped in this isolated corner of the universe. The huge *Enterprise* was an insignificant spot, a parasitic white shape alongside it.

"A thousand cathedrals all thrown together and then they added star-drive," whispered an awed McCoy. "Tossed all together and lit like a Christmas tree."

"Can it really be a starship?" murmured Uhura softly.

Spock's reply was equally hushed. "The probability is ... considerable."

Vast arches and flying buttresses of multicolored metal and plastic soared up and out, racing in and around metallic spirals and pyramids. Here and there, gracefully designed yet massive metal pods nestled at regular intervals amid cradling arms of silver and gold and iridescent blue. Faery arms of spun alloy.

The race that had built this vessel was a race of artisans as well as engineers, poets as well as shipwrights.

"Bring us in, Mr. Sulu. Mr. Sulu?"

The lieutenant seemed to shake himself awake. "Aye, sir." He touched controls, and the *Enterprise* responded. The intricate gleaming tapestry began to move closer and then past them.

Under Sulu's skillful hands, the *Enterprise* drifted

deeper into the tangle of alien crossbeams and spars. He adjusted speed and they drifted towards what seemed to be a major pod.

"It's got to be a starship!" McCoy muttered. "But, Aesculapius, the size of it!"

"True, Bones," Kirk agreed and then gestured, "but it seems that neither size nor beauty renders it invulnerable. Or maybe to something else, it wasn't so beautiful. Look!"

As they continued their inspection, it became clear that despite its massive bulk, some time in the past the alien ship had undergone stresses and strains of as yet unknown but undeniably powerful origin.

Arches and soaring spans of binding metal were torn and scorched—bent unnaturally in some places, sliced in half in others. The huge pods exhibited the most obvious, ominous signs of disaster. They were lined with rows of odd, hexagonal-shaped ports. All were cold, dark.

Dead.

Every pod was damaged. There were no exceptions. The metal floated easily in space, bloated with ruptures and tears. Deep gashes split one pod like a chrome grape.

"She was probably pulled in like we were," murmured Kirk. He didn't voice the attendant thought. Had this total destruction taken place before the alien starship was gathered in by the negative sun's gravity—or after?

And if the latter, why? More importantly, how?

Two surprises from outside were enough for any one station, but Uhura was destined to get yet a third. Idly adjusting receivers and amplifiers, she suddenly threw the sound of the secondary signal—the signal that came from this dead enigma—into the bridge again.

But it was different now. More of a stutter than a moan. And while there were no reasons, no facts to support it, everyone sensed that the strange call was now more urgent, more insistent than before.

"Confirmation, sir, final," she said excitedly. "I *thought* that signal was coming from the alien. Not only is there no longer any question about it, but somehow the transmitter, at least, has reacted to our presence! That's the only reason I can think of to explain this sudden change in broadcast pattern."

"I have secondary confirmation, Captain," added Spock, his eyebrows rising again, "and I should agree. But—it isn't possible. That ship is utterly, unequivocally, dead. All life-support sensors read negative. All ship-support sensors read the same. No energy is present. Temperature on board the alien is identical to that of open space—absolute zero. I have no reason to even faintly support the contention that there is life aboard . . . biological or mechanical."

"Also, there is no evidence of any stored energy capable of generating these radio emissions. I read only a slight magnetic flux—probably normal for the vessel's metal."

"Yet you reconfirm Uhura's readings—that the signal is coming from the ship?"

Spock seemed reluctant to restate his position, but, "I have no choice, Captain. That is likewise what the sensors read."

"That doesn't make sense, Mr. Spock."

The science officer's reply was drier than usual. "We find ourselves in complete agreement, Captain. Yet," he paused briefly, "that is the case."

"You're positive?"

"Probability ninety-nine point seven, Captain."

"Ummmm." Kirk leaned back, drumming a mildly obscene ditty with his fingers on one arm of the command chair. Pursuing a confessed paradox was going to get them nowhere. Better try another tack.

"Can you identify the design of the ship or its composition, Mr. Spock?"

"Negative to both, Captain," Spock replied after a glance at the computer readout. "The readings I have so far on the alloy itself—barring actual analytical confirmation from a specimen of same—indicate a material both harder and lighter than any registered in the ship's library. As for the design, it is not a recorded type." He hesitated, glanced back at the readout.

"Something else, Mr. Spock?"

"Also, Captain, silicon dating or the vessel's spectra in-

dicates that it has been floating in orbit here for . . ." he
checked the computer figures one last time, ". . . for
slightly more and not less than three hundred million terran years."

There was a concerted gasp from the bridge personnel.
Everyone's attention was drawn back to the screen. Back
to the delicate arches, to the dreamlike design—alien in
both pattern and function to the solid, prosaic shape of
the *Enterprise*.

"I should think, then, that that precludes our chances
of finding any survivors aboard," Kirk murmured.

"I couldn't have put it better myself, Captain," agreed
Spock.

"I just know that it's beautiful," put in Uhura, half-
defiantly. "To have put such grace and perfection of form
into something as functional as a starship—I wish I could
have known the race that built it."

"Beauty may have nothing to do with it, Lieutenant,"
suggested Spock conversationally. "The design may
merely conform to their own conceptions of spatial dynam-
ics."

She turned back to her instruments, an expression of
distaste coming over her perfect features.

"I might have guessed you'd say something like that,
Spock."

"Don't give it a thought, Uhura," chipped in McCoy
quickly. "According to his own system of spatial dynam-
ics, Spock probably finds your form purely functional,
too. Don't you, Spock?"

Sulu grinned, and even Kirk was distracted enough to
smile.

Spock's reply barely hinted at mild distress. "It is very
easy to tell when you are joking, Doctor—which is most
of the time. It is when your statements make absolutely no
sense—which is most of the time."

While the byplay continued behind him, Kirk let his attention drift back to the picture of the alien starship. He
envied the long-dead commander. And yet there was a
hint of unease back of all the admiration.

What could have happened to so totally destroy such a
magnificent vessel, with all its unknown potentialities and

abilities? Certainly it must have possessed defensive powers commensurate with its size. "A civilization advanced enough to build such a craft—three hundred million years ago! Man wasn't even an idea then in the mind of nature," he murmured.

"A second or two in the span of eternity, Jim," McCoy commented, switching abruptly from the silly to the sublime.

Sometimes McCoy's comments grew wearisome, even annoying. But when he was right, he was the rightest person on the ship.

Kirk sighed. "All right, Spock. There's got to be an answer to this. You read no power from the vessel now. Any indication what its power source might have been?"

"No, Captain. There is apparently something new and undetectable at work here, capable of avoiding even the most delicate sensor pickup. But this far from any star with a planetary system, it goes without saying that they possessed some form of warp-drive. A most efficient one, beyond doubt, judging from the size of the craft."

Kirk continued to study the vast alien ship. As usual, the sudden flash of insight that would solve all and make him appear the most brilliant spacer since O'Morion didn't occur.

He had no business ordering what he was about to order. Every second should have been devoted to extricating the *Enterprise* from its present perilous position. Still, the lure of the incredible vessel was too strong to ignore. He hesitated. At least he could make one last check.

"Mr. Spock, how is the computer coming on the computation for a slingshot course?"

Spock consulted his viewer. "It appears it will take some time yet, Captain, for all the variables to be considered and an optimum program to be devised."

That settled it. He rose and spoke firmly.

"We'll board her, then. Scotty, Bones—you'll come with us. Life-support belts, of course. Lieutenant Uhura, you're in command. Sulu, have the transporter room stand by."

"Yes, sir," Sulu replied as he moved to notify the transporter chief. The four officers were already heading for the elevator.

"Captain," said Spock, "may I inquire as to your reasons for boarding the alien?"

"Nothing extraordinary, Mr. Spock. We have the time. Curiosity. Plain old ordinary human curiosity."

"That is what I thought. However, if that expression of exclusivity is intended for my benefit, Captain, you ought to know by now that it's misplaced."

"Why, Spock!" McCoy exclaimed, rising to the challenge, "don't tell me that you're subject to an emotion like curiosity!"

"Your evaluation of the phenomenon is typically inaccurate, Doctor. Curiosity is a natural, logical function of the higher mind—not one of the baser emotions."

"That all depends on how you choose to interpret it," McCoy countered. "Now . . ."

The argument was continuing full force as they entered the transporter room. Transporter Chief Kyle was at the console, waiting for them. The console itself emitted a barely audible hum, an indication that it was prepared and ready to perform its usual functions.

Kyle had also removed and checked four life-support belts from the nearby lockers. Kirk, Spock, McCoy, and Scott buckled them on, each double-checking his own and then throwing the activating switches. Each passed before Kyle's console for a last, mechanical check. Kyle's voice read out the results.

"Captain . . . check. Commander Spock . . . check. Lt. Commander Scott . . . okay. Lt. Commander McCoy . . . check." He looked up. "All belts operational, Captain."

"Thank you, Mr. Kyle."

"If you'll take your places, sirs. . . ." A lime-yellow aura now surrounded each man—a comforting, vital field put out by the life-support belts. They stepped up into the transporter alcove and took their places on four separate transporter disks.

"Ready, Captain," warned Kyle.

"Ready, Chief," Kirk replied, then grinned. "Try not to materialize us inside any solid objects, hmmm?"

Kyle essayed a slight grin at the old joke. Safety overrides on all transporters made such occurrences quite impossible.

"Energize, Chief," instructed Kirk.

Kyle carefully brought the necessary levers up, keeping a watchful eye on the vast array of monitoring instrumentation. A familiar, part-musical, tinkling hum filled the transporter room as the alcove was energized. The bodies of the four men slowly diffused, as if seen through squinted eyes in early morning . . . until they became four cylinders of multicolored particles glowing on the platforms.

Kyle hit a switch, drew the four levers rapidly down.

He was alone in the transporter room.

Four pillars of speckled fire appeared on the cold surface of the largest pod of the alien starship. The pillars faded quickly, to be replaced by the frighteningly fragile figures of three humans and a Vulcan. Each stood bathed in soft lime-yellow light.

Spock was the first to survey their harsh surroundings. They were standing next to one of the huge, dark, hexagonal ports. Just beyond the port was an enormous, gaping hole, a black pit fringed with torn, twisted metal clawing at empty space. Clear indication that whatever cataclysm had ruptured the skin of the pod had come from within.

As soon as everyone had recovered fully from the effects of transporter dislocation, they began to move toward the forced opening. All paused briefly by the dark port. Spock ran the thin force-field of the life-support system under his heel over the black, glassy surface.

"The six-sided shape of the port suggests a similarity to the natural designs of certain terran insects. The honeycombs of bees, for example, where the individual bee cells possess a similar shape. Such a similarity is, naturally, purely superficial. To read any possibilities into it would be unreasonable."

Kirk knelt and tried to peer through the thick glass—which wasn't necessarily glass, or thick. In any case, it was like staring at an onyx mirror. If anything remained inside the pod, they'd never get a look at it this way.

Engineer Scott was standing near one of the torn flanges of metal, running his hands over it. He had his face so close to it that the force-field over his nose was nearly touching.

"Would ye look at this, now!" he whistled in surprise. His lifebelt radio carried the eerie disembodied sound to his companions.

"What is it, Scotty?" Kirk rose and moved toward him from the unrevealing port.

"It's this metal, sir. I don't know much about terran insects, but I do know metal. This stuff wasn't cast or rolled or flextruded. And it's got a faint but definite *grain*, like fine grains in good wood." He looked disbelievingly at Kirk.

"I'm willin' to bet, sir, that this metal was made by being drawn out into long, very thin filaments and then formed into required shapes. There's layer on layer on layer of 'em right here in this one small section. Like laminating in plastics, only on a much finer scale." He tapped the metal silently.

"The way a spider spins its web," Kirk mused.

"If you will, sir," continued Scott. "Such a method of metal formin'—even with our own alloys—would make for material far stronger than anything known."

Spock had his phaser out. The brilliant beam of the tiny weapon lanced across space and sliced free a small segment of the metal. Spock caught the sample before momentum imparted by the phaser could shove it away, examined it closely.

"Lighter and stronger than anything we have now," he whispered, echoing an earlier reading." Then he looked in turn at McCoy, Scott, Kirk. "If this can be analyzed, Captain—"

"And duplicated," Scott added.

"I know, I know," Kirk admitted. He didn't want to put a damper on their enthusiasm—he felt pretty much the same—but they were in no position to get carried away by *any* discovery.

"Providing, however, that we're not trapped here ourselves, for some other unfortunate starship crew to stumble across a hundred million years from now."

Stepping back along the graceful metal beam that emerged from this section of the torn pod, he moved to get a better view of the rest of the alien vessel. Staring upwards he scanned the fronds of the metal jungle, eyed the other shredded and shattered pod-shapes.

Nearby, one thin soaring arch, as delicate as the finest example of the wood-carver's art, dangled crookedly, distorted by unimaginable stresses in the far-distant past.

"Look," he instructed the others. "Every pod—every one. Notice any similarity?"

For a change, McCoy was the first to reply.

"They've *all* been burst open, Jim. Funny—there doesn't seem to be an intact one on the entire ship. Maybe on the other side, but . . ."

"Aye," acknowledged Scott, "and all from the inside, too. But we already saw that."

"Must have been some accident," the doctor added, "to get every pod."

Spock replied without looking, choosing instead to speak while studying the ruins of the ship.

"Accidents seldom operate according to a system, Dr. McCoy. The destruction here is too regular, too obviously managed for 'accident' to be given as cause. No, I believe we must give serious consideration to the alternative possibility that the crew of this vessel voluntarily destroyed her—and, incidentally, perhaps, themselves."

Leave it to Spock, thought Kirk, to voice what all of them were thinking but none could say.

They stood there—four insignificant animate forms, on the skin of a starship tens of millions of years in advance of anything their own civilization could produce—and considered what threat might be serious enough to prompt her crew to suicide.

Dwelling on morbidity brought no answers. Kirk started off toward the beckoning black cave and the others followed, striding with the aid of belt-gravity across the smooth hull. Without breaking stride he brought out his communicator, flipped the cover back.

"Kirk to *Enterprise*."

"*Enterprise*," came the prompt reply. Kirk was gratified. That gal would make a fine captain someday. "Uhura speaking."

"Lieutenant, are you still receiving radio emissions from this vessel?"

"When did you develop telepathy, Captain?" came the startled reply. "I was about to call down when you checked in. It ceased broadcasting the moment you stepped aboard."

Kirk considered this.

"Whatever machinery is still somehow operating on board this craft, Captain," theorized Spock, "is also sensitive." Kirk nodded agreement, spoke into the communicator again.

"Thank you, Uhura. Inform Chief Kyle to lock on with the transporter and be ready to yank us out of here on a second's notice."

There was a pause while Uhura relayed the necessary information.

"Expecting trouble, sir?"

"No, Lieutenant. But we're going to try and enter the ship. There may be surprises other than finicky radio transmissions, something of a less indifferent nature."

Another pause, and then a second voice came over the compact speaker.

"Kyle here. Don't worry, Captain, I've got all four of you right on frequency. And I'm not budging from this console until you're all back on board."

Kirk smiled, closed the communicator.

"Sounds like the chief," smiled McCoy. Another few steps had brought them to the edge of the gaping, metal-fringed cavern.

Kirk spent a long moment examining the dim, shadowy interior. Clearly nothing was alive here. He swung lightly over the edge. Scott followed. McCoy stepped aside and gestured inward.

"After you, Spock."

"Why, Doctor, don't tell me that you, a man of science, are afraid of the dark?"

"Very funny, Spock—say, that wasn't intended to be—no, that's impossible. Vulcans don't joke."

"Joke, Doctor?" Spock's expression was unreadable.

"Oh, well," McCoy sighed. "Hope springs eternal." He followed the science officer into the abyss.

They moved slowly, carefully down the wide passageway. If necessary, the glow of their life-support belts would have been sufficient to see one another by. As it developed, that glow wasn't needed.

Faint light issued from long panels of translucent, polyethylenelike material inlaid in the walls of the airlock—for such it clearly was. Or had once been. Both air and at least the outer lock had long since departed—the air by natural forces, the lock by apparently unnatural ones.

Spock studied one of the luminescent panels. He couldn't see a tube, a bulb, or a strip beneath it. The light seemed to come from the plastic material itself, but he couldn't be sure.

"Something in the ship is still, somehow, generating power that our sensors were unable to record, Captain. Or else there are other devices that somehow generate their own power—as these light panels seem to do."

"Don't look a gift horse in the mouth, Spock. It's a damnsight easier than moving with only belt-light to see by."

They continued deeper into the tunnel. Eventually they came up short against what appeared to be a solid wall of metal. It blocked further passage very thoroughly. Initial inspection produced nothing but disappointment.

It was Scott, who first noticed the slightly brighter stream of light up near the "ceiling." Sure enough, the metal there was bent. Some titanic force had wrenched at the very structure of this inner lock.

"Some kind of emergency shutoff seems to have been in action here," Scott guessed. "Energy was operating on a tremendous scale. It would have had to be, to bend this alloy like that." He nodded up at the revealing gap. "This passage is big enough for one of the Enterprise's shuttlecraft to fit in."

Kirk put out a hand and touched the dull metal. He couldn't feel it, of course—the force-field blocked the sense of touch—which was just as well, since the metal was as cold as open space. His hand would have frozen to it.

He knew the door was solid because something halted the progress of his palm. The gesture was more hopeful than anticipatory. As expected, nothing happened when he shoved. The enormous lock didn't budge.

"Let's try up near where the top buckled," he suggested. "If it's only jammed and not really locked, we might be able to jar it loose."

He and Scott took out their hand phasers. Two beams of incandescence began to play about the top of the lock.

Two minutes of concentrated beaming, however, produced nothing more than a slight red glow in the affected area.

"Useless," he murmured, watching the red glow fade along with all hopes of entering the ship.

"Captain."

The two men put their phasers away.

"What is it, Mr. Spock?" Kirk squinted. Spock was off on the other side of the passageway.

"I believe I may have had some luck, Captain."

"I hope so, Spock. We haven't. We may have to bring the *Enterprise*'s main phasers to bear in here. I'd hate to do that. Either we'll surely damage whatever's inside—the main batteries aren't as delicate as Bones' cutters—or else we won't be able to cut through at all."

They moved over to where Spock was waiting. He said nothing, only pointed upward.

About three meters off the floor was a large square panel, recessed into the wall of the tunnel. Three hexagonal-shaped plastic plates were set into the recess.

"I think, Captain, that that may be a key. Probability would suggest some form of manual backup system to operate any airlock."

"I agree, Spock." Kirk studied the panel, made an experimental jump. "There's only one problem—artificial gravity seems to be in full operation here. For the moment, our key is out of reach. Someone can beam back aboard and bring back a . . ."

"I do not believe that will be necessary, Captain." Spock moved to the curving wall and braced himself against the metal. "If you will climb onto my shoulders, you should be able to reach the panel."

"Isn't science wonderful?" murmured McCoy.

It took Kirk, a trained gymnast and tumbler, only a second or two. Then he was securely braced on the Vulcan's shoulders. Even so, the recessed panel was still over his head. But by straining his arm he could manage to reach all three hexagonal plates.

"I always said you were a supportive influence, Spock," ventured McCoy.

"And I've always felt your humor was in execrable taste, Doctor." Spock's voice barely hinted at the strain of keeping Kirk's weight on his shoulders. "However I feel that in all honesty I must revise my opinion of your puns."

"Well, it's about time! I always knew you'd come around, Spock."

"They are," the science officer continued, "not merely bad. They are atrocious." McCoy's expression fell.

Kirk pressed firmly on the nearest plastic hexagon. It sank inward under his fingers, but nothing else happened. Trying the one to its left produced a similar lack of results. When he hit the third panel, however, the plastic suddenly pulsed with a soft green glow.

The brilliant reaction from something three hundred million years "dead" was startling—so much so that Kirk nearly fell.

"Careful, Captain," Spock admonished, tightening his grip on Kirk's legs. "I can support you like this for a long time, but if you insist on shifting your weight, well, I'm not an acrobat."

"Don't worry, Mr. Spock. I'm the one who'll end up falling. I don't plan to, not even in this light gravity." He kept his hand on the depressed disk and was rewarded with a faint but massive grinding sound.

"It's movin', Captain!" shouted Scott.

Sure enough, there'd been a slight hint of motion from the massive lock door. And the space near its top admitting light from somewhere within had grown a little wider. But the grinding stopped immediately and the green light faded from the disk.

"Try again, Captain," Spock suggested. Kirk pressed the disk once more. The glow returned. So did the grinding noise. He kept the disk forced down, trying to watch the lock door at the same time.

He heard a deep and echoing ripping sound, as of ancient joints and bolts giving way. The massive door shuddered, started to swing wide on unseen hinges ... then stopped. This time not all Kirk's jabs on the disk could move it.

But there was a gap between door and tunnel wall now wide enough for a man to slip through.

"That's good enough, Spock! Coming down." He jumped carefully clear of his second's shoulders and moved to the new opening.

They had seen nothing so far to indicate that any excessive caution was required. Nonetheless, Kirk stepped softly as he edged through the gap. Spock followed, with Scott and McCoy bringing up the rear. The captain's last real fear was eliminated when they were all inside and the gigantic lock door failed to slam shut behind them.

The interior of the chamber in which they now found themselves was built on an enormous, inhuman scale. The walls were the color of pale chalcedony, dull and waxlike whites and blues. They curved upward and outward, forming a room vaguely hexagonal in pattern. Apparently the six-sided format was repeated throughout the interior of the vessel as well as in the construction of the superstructure.

The walls and sections of floor were lined with shattered, smashed machines of unknown, indefinable purpose. It was unlikely their purposes would ever be divined. Even the smallest device partook of the same feathery, lacelike design as the great ship itself. It was almost as though the builders had selected the internal structure of a leaf as their pattern for interstellar craft.

Some shapes—more solid, less ethereal of form—were still intact. And still operating ... or at least dormant. They pulsed with different shades and blends of the visible spectrum. Violet and umber, emerald green and deep maroon and a light, pastel pink—each seemingly too beautiful to be functional.

The men moved toward the center of the room, where a monstrous amorphous shape squatted like a jeweled toad.

From its top, graceful appendages radiated roofward in all directions—wands of flexible crystal. The four men moved closer.

As they advanced, the crystalline strands began to move. Slowly, gently, swaying to the ebb of some unseen tide. As the strands moved they were accompanied by a strangely melodic, somehow nocturnal music.

McCoy murmured, "I heard something like that, once. Not exactly the same, but close. Ever hear electric cello, Jim?"

"Close, close," Kirk agreed. "I wouldn't swear to any similarity, though. You know me, Bones, I'm more partial to classical stuff."

They stopped next to the enigmatic structure. When they halted, the floating fronds also stilled, the haunting music fading out in a last, trilling pianissimo.

"What do you make of it, Spock?" Kirk asked. As he spoke, the translucent limbs fluttered slightly and invisible fingers ran ever so lightly over a faraway harp.

"Look here, Captain," interrupted Scott before Spock could answer. He was pointing to the upper surface of the stocky construction.

A thin, sparkling band of pink light had suddenly appeared around the upper trunk of the main body. Spock made a quick reading with his tricorder.

"Captain, it's registering energy output. Quite weak, but definite."

"Still functioning, then," mused Kirk softly, "after all these millennia. The lock door I can understand—it *would* operate off any oddball, emergency power source. But this thing?"

Spock was circling the object, constantly consulting his tricorder. He was shaking his head as he rejoined them.

"I am still getting tricorder readings, Captain." When he spoke there was music and movement in the room again. "I would hazard an opinion that those strange appendages are accumulators, receptors that pick up any faint form of kinetic energy—motion, movement in the air from sound waves . . . our voices . . . anything."

"It absorbs this energy and metamorphoses it, returning it or 'playing it back' in at least two readily observable ways. As motion in its 'arms' and as music ... if those sounds are indeed an alien conception of music."

"Yes, but what is its function?" Kirk pressed, staring at the wands. They threw his words back at him and added a lithe tune.

"As to that, Captain, your guess is as good as mine. This could be anything," and he gestured at the shape, "from an energy-acceptance station for the starship's engines to a recreation area for her crew. We do not have enough information to deduce."

"It gives me the creeps," announced McCoy firmly. It wasn't a flip evaluation, either. "I feel like something that ought to be dead is watching us." Scott looked equally uneasy all of a sudden. Machines were his province. He knew them better than most people, but this thing—

"Aye, Captain, I feel it, too."

"A standard physiological symptom of latent primal superstition." Spock said. "The fear of primitive peoples confronting something utterly incomprehensible to them."

Kirk was studying the rest of the silent chamber. He spoke idly.

"Compared to the beings that built this craft, we *are* primitive peoples. You too, Mr. Spock."

"I did not mean to imply otherwise, Captain. Merely to attempt an evaluation of—"

"All right, all right, never mind, Spock. Let's keep moving."

He pointed to the far side of the chamber where another door waited.

## III

Whereas the inner airlock door had been a single massive plate of unadorned metal, this portal was both more elaborately designed and more formal-looking. It was decorative as well as practical. The flat surface was seamed by triple lines, forming three triangles, each engraved deeply with alien words and cryptography. To the men of the *Enterprise* they were so many scratches.

Spock located another recess with its three inserted hexagonal disks.

But when he depressed them, nothing happened. All four stared at the seemingly impenetrable barrier for a while.

"Of course!" blurted Scott suddenly, as the others turned. "The other door was bent, damaged, so only one disk was enough to operate it. Or maybe the circuitry was jammed together. But three triangles—three disks. Press them all at the same time, Mr. Spock."

"Quite so, Mr. Scott," concurred Spock, sharing in the chief engineer's revelation.

His hand was not quite wide enough to cover all three disks, but both hands managed the trick neatly. This feat gave them some idea of the size of the starship's crew members, or of their manipulative digits, anyway. Spock pressed in.

The three disks glowed green. Seconds later the three sections of door slid back silently, disappearing into walls, roof, and floor. Another huge chamber opened beyond.

The interior of the pod was circular in design, with

huge rooms spaced around a common core, and they were walking around it. This particular chamber was lined with a long row of the dark, hexagonal ports they'd seen from outside. Whether it was from starlight they admitted or the presence of more of the ubiquitous plastic strips, the light here was much brighter.

"No, Captain," mused Spock as they discussed the continuing puzzle of the strange illumination. "I think the light has been on in here all the time."

"Why couldn't we see in through the ports, then, from out—Oh, of course." Kirk answered his own question. "One-way ports, to protect the observer from external light and other radiation sources."

They moved deeper into the long, curving chamber. One interior wall was dominated by a huge reflective shape. It resembled a giant convex mirror and was also six-sided in form, though greatly stretched-out. Objects with even stranger patterns—weird instrumentation and peculiar machinery—lined all the visible walls and dominated rank on rank of high, slanted consoles.

There was something else unusual, more unusual than any individual piece of apparatus.

The destruction that had blasted the rest of the starship, including the room they'd just left, was not in evidence. Whatever catastrophe had torn the great vessel asunder had passed over this room.

As they moved further into the chamber and close to specific instruments, lights began to appear, glowing, emanating from scattered dials and panels and hidden strips of plastic.

"Proximity activation," noted Scott absently. "Huh-oh . . . look there." They stopped, turned.

The gigantic mirror, which was doubtless anything but so simple a device, began to exhibit a milky opalescence. Colors commenced to flow and drift and blend across its surface. A moment later there was more music. But this was quite different from the sounds produced by the octopoidal machine in the other chamber. They were more rhythmic, insistent and yet soothing.

They moved toward it, curious. Spock began to adjust

his tricorder, preparatory to taking some preliminary readings.

"A most intriguing phenome . . ."

The gentle light on the clustered console to Kirk's right abruptly exploded in brilliant green. A lurid, blinding emerald flare bathed them all. Formerly stolid, calm music changed suddenly to an enraged percussive clamoring. An enormous outpouring of emotion that even over three hundred million years and unfathomable differences in shape and physiology still sounded unmistakably like an alarm.

Behind them the three segments of the tripartite portal slammed silently shut. McCoy took a couple of steps toward it, slowed, stopped when he realized the futility of the gesture.

The light dimmed; the music ceased.

They were trapped in the cyclopean cave.

There were the three familiar disks set in a familiar recess to the left of the doorway. McCoy sauntered over slowly and depressed the three plastic plates. Lightly at first, then with all his strength. Then he tried them in various combinations. All attempts produced equal results— none at all. The door remained resolutely closed, as obstinate as the dead star circling below them. Not even the faint light appeared from within the disks.

Various imprecations and comments on the dubious parentage of the door's designers also failed to have a salutory effect.

"Somehow I didn't think it would work, Bones." Kirk smiled grimly. "Analysis, Mr. Spock?"

Spock consulted the all-purpose tricorder once more, wishing instead for the mythical terran supercomputer JWG. Wishing was not logical, but under the circumstances, he permitted himself the tiny private deviation. The tricorder singularly uninformative.

"Nothing available on whatever activated the door mechanism, Captain. But an atmosphere has been supplied now." He sounded surprised. "It approaches Earthnormal. Shall we deactivate life-support belts? We may be here for a while and this gives us an opportunity to conserve the power supply since we can't return to the *Enterprise* for recharging."

Kirk hesitated. Force-fields could be more of a problem than a benefit at the damndest times, but . . .

"No, Spock. This is just a bit too neat, too easy. That door could open again as fast as it closed. Whatever established an atmosphere in here might not have had the foresight to do the same in the other room. No, we'll keep our life-support systems on." He flipped open his communicator, eyed the now ominous walls uncertainly.

"*Enterprise,* do you read me? Mr. Sulu?" He paused, tried again. "Lieutenant Uhura, acknowledge. This is the captain speaking."

A faint, rhythmic humming was the only sound the speaker in the compact unit produced—a normal blank receptor wave. That proved the communicator was operating.

"No use, Captain," said Spock, still working with the tricorder. "Some sort of blanket interference has been set up. Its efficiency approaches totality." He looked up from the 'corder.

"I do not like this at all, Captain."

McCoy had ambled back to rejoin them.

"You always did have this marvelous ability for understatement, Spock. A gigantic alien zombie could come crashing through the near wall, spewing fire and dripping venom from poisonous fangs, and you'd sum the situation up by declaring that its intentions were other than benign!"

Kirk noticed that Scott had his phaser out. "What are you going to do with that, Scotty? We can't cut our way out any more than we could cut our way in."

"No, sir," the engineer admitted. "Not exactly."

"You've got an idea, Scotty. Don't keep us guessing."

"Well, sir, these walls are tough, I'll give you that." He gestured towards the trisected door with the phaser. "But those control disks don't look like they're made of any-thin' near as strong a material. If I can burn through the covering plates and short the controls—assumin' they're shortable—there's no reason why the door shouldn't release."

"It's a good thought, Scotty," Kirk confessed. "I don't like being destructive, but . . . Give it a try."

Scott walked over and eyed the recessed disks briefly. He lined up the phaser on the lowest one, carefully set the power level, and pressed the trigger.

Nothing happened.

He tried again, turning up the power all the way. This time he produced a very faint red glow which quickly faded and disappeared.

At a sudden thought Kirk pulled out his communicator again. This time he didn't try to activate it. Instead, he turned it over and checked the power telltale set in the base.

"No energy rating. Something's drained them. Blanket interference my eye! Something's at work in here that drinks energy like a sponge." His eyes darted around the innocent-seeming chamber, saw—as expected—nothing.

"And whatever it is, it's selective. These panels and dials are still glowing, still activated. I'm surprised this even picked up a carrier wave, before."

McCoy had his own comm unit out, checked it and then repeated the check with his phaser.

"Mine too, Jim."

"And mine," Spock added. "But not the tricorder." He made his own survey of the silent room. "Odd."

"So we're stuck," said McCoy unsubtly. "No communications and no weapons . . . no way of telling Kyle to pull us out of this." He jammed the useless instruments back in his belt.

"Only for the moment, Bones. Things are happening awfully fast here. They might happen in our favor any moment. We'd better be ready to take advantage of them if we get a chance. You miss a lot mooning over current disappointments. For example, notice anything new?"

They all searched the chamber. Creamy opalescence still washed across the face of the convex mirror. Lights still flickered and stuttered from different instruments.

"I see. Everything's returned to normal." McCoy studied the mirror. "Or at least, what was passing for normal when we came in." He paused a moment, listening. "Even the music's back—if that's what it is."

Kirk noticed the large, hexagonal dais in the center of the room. They had just been passing it when everything had gone crazy. Now, staring at it intently for the first time, he kicked himself mentally for not noticing the similarity before. Despite its size and shape it bore an unmistakable, if faint, resemblance to another smaller, more familiar object . . . his own command chair.

Recessed knobs, oddly curled levers, and triple-disk controls lined the slanted face of consoles inside the "chair," along with a vast array of multicolored, winking dials and band indicators. There were markings over the transparent dials and plates that might have been instructions, directions. Whatever secrets they held were locked up in a long-extinct alphabet and mathematical system.

"Control and navigation instrumentation, maybe," he mused. He turned to scan the room, suddenly seeing it in a new light.

"I'll bet this was the ship's bridge." He touched the peculiarly formed seat. "The captain must have sat here, in this same chair—eons ago." He stood on tiptoes and let himelf down gently into the seat. Whatever the nature of his long-dead alien counterpart, one thing was certain, their backsides had differing configurations.

Spock was fiddling with the tricorder as he circled the command chair.

"I don't think so, Captain. The source of the interference is here, somewhere. Also, various aspects of construction taken together with certain readings lead me to believe that this was not a part of the vessel's original equipment. It seems much more like something that was made up for a special occasion—'jury-rigged' I think you call it. To handle an emergency, for example.

"One thing is certain . . . it's generating all kinds of energy patterns. I suspect that the signal which activated the door came from here, too."

"Sure some sort of automatics were designed to seal off this room," agreed Scott, suddenly uneasy. "But seal it off from what?"

"Not from us, obviously," added McCoy.

"This ship, despite its size and probable power," Spock continued, "has been all but totally destroyed. Even the last chamber we were in. But this room, these instruments, this console—especially this console—they remain intact.

"Something, gentlemen, once came aboard this ship. Something formidable enough to not only destroy it here, but enough to cause her crew to commit suicide . . . yet leave this one last room intact. As a precaution, I should think."

"But the door closed when we entered here," protested Scott. "Surely we didn . . ." He stopped and his mouth gaped. "Oh, come on now, Spock! No known form of life could survive three hundred million years of exposure to naked space!"

"Quite right, Mr. Scott," agreed Spock grimly. "No known form of life.

McCoy interrupted them all.

"Jim, Spock, Scotty . . . the door . . . !" They whirled as one.

In the center of the still tightly closed portal, lines of glowing emerald energy, shading occasionally to aquamarine, now to deep olive, were playing freely across the metal surface.

"No," McCoy whispered, taking a step backwards.

Spock studied tricorder readings and spoke without emotion.

"Something is trying to get in here, Captain. The interference energy put out and directed by this console is reacting with another outside energy source of unknown proportions and capabilities. The flux that is the result of this interaction is now visible on the surface of the door."

"Will it hold?" Kirk asked. Spock nodded slowly.

"If the energy involved holds at present levels and does not increase."

Kirk studied the door. It was hard to turn away from that threatening, shockingly silent conflict of energies. But he forced himself to, to look down and study the alien controls. Somewhere in the maze of dials and switches designed for digits other than fingers there had to be a clue to what was happening. Something, anything at all, to give them a hint of what they might be up against.

On a hunch and with a lack of any real information to proceed on (not a very promising base) he began pressing in disks, moving switches as best he could with clumsy hands. For a while nothing happened. Then, when he accidentally nudged a spiral-shaped knob, the lights in the console began to intensify. Spock murmured something, and Kirk glanced up at his science officer.

"The mirror-thing, Captain." Kirk turned so that he could see the huge, hexagonal reflector.

It was beginning to pulse softly. The rippling waves of diffuse color started to flow more rapidly across its shifting surface. The mirror shuddered, turned to face them on some kind of hidden swivel mounting.

For a moment the four of them were reflected in the gleaming, curved material, enlarged and grotesquely distorted.

"What is it, Jim?" McCoy demanded. "What's it doing?"

"I don't know, Bones." Kirk tried to watch the mirror and handle the console at the same time. Something had activated the mirror this far. Very well. His hands played over controls as yet untouched. After a few moments the colors started to fade, the mirror itself to brighten.

Then the chaotic display of color solidified, coalesced into blurred images fluttering across the screen. That's what it was, a screen! And sound emanated from it now, too ... a husky chittering like the song of a gigantic cricket. But the sound was much more varied, much richer in invention. Somewhere behind those sounds there was a guiding intelligence.

A picture began to form in the mirror-screen. The image sharpened. In the background was a control room of some sort. A familiar control room.

The control room they were in now.

More interesting still was the creature that dominated the screen. It was insectlike but not ugly. Its surface features were smooth, streamlined—not spiky, boney, or sharp. It was difficult to get an idea of its true size because of the way it dominated the mirror-screen. It must have been sitting very close to the visual pickup. But it was clear that it was much bigger than any man.

Big enough to need the two huge doorways they'd encountered thus far. Big enough to make use of a ship this size. Big enough so that each pod might be quarters for a single crew member.

Not big enough to prevent its destruction.

Now they could match up the strange sounds coming from speakers behind the screen with the being's mouth movements. There was a definite tone of urgency in its peculiar, rasping words. It seemed—though it was hard to tell due to vast differences in voice-box construction—that some of its message was being repeated, over and over.

Kirk finally broke the silence that had settled over the little group. The creature on the screen didn't react to the sound of his voice. If there was any lingering doubt about that, there was none now. They were watching a recorded message, and none cared to think how old it might be.

"Could be the ship's log," he thought out loud. "Or a warning. Or a religious service, or instructions for game playing, or music lessons."

"I think not, Captain," said Spock. "This preparation and care hints at more than mere frivolity."

"True . . . there, there's that same collection of sounds again!" Kirk insisted. "It's repeating itself, all right—at least part of the time."

McCoy murmured, "A message from three million centuries ago."

"It is possible, it seems," nodded Spock. "That much of their amazing technology has survived." He was working with the tricorder again.

Kirk divided his attention between his busy science officer and the strange alien on the mirror-screen.

"Can you get anything out of this, Spock?"

"I may be able to affect a translation," he replied. "The basic voice pattern does not exhibit any impossible aural characteristics. Perhaps we are deceived as to its potential complexity by sheer age."

A sudden change seemed to come over the voice of the ancient speaker. His speech was louder now, more insistent. McCoy glanced back at the triple door. Scott followed the doctor's glance with a worried one of his own.

The green and light-blue bands of energy sparking across its surface were thicker, less intermittent than before. Whatever was at work on the incredibly tough alloy was definitely working its way through.

"Hurry up, Spock."

"Patience, Doctor." He activated some switches on the

tricorder. Leaving the compact instrument, he started to scan the console, examining switches and dials.

Eventually he seemed to find what he was looking for. He removed the tricorder from his shoulder and placed it carefully on the panel, setting it on top of a small six-sided grid set into the metal. A last switch depressed on the tricorder and then he stepped back, turning to watch the screen.

Instantly, the voice of the alien started coming from the tricorder speaker instead of from the mirror-screen. The chittering sounds began to seem less garbled, more comprehensible. Blank spaces in the speech replaced chitters, where the tricorder's marvelous abilities were unable to translate delicacies of alien syntax.

"Danger . . . (more chittering sounds) . . . star . . . drawn to it . . ."

Spock reached up and made some final, fine adjustments to the 'corder. The voice was suddenly clear and understandable in the huge chamber.

". . . Rather than carry this malevolent life form to other worlds," came the voice from across time, "we have decided to destroy our own ship. The Thing had been trapped here by the tremendous gravity-well of the dead sun. So it must remain. So, sadly, must we. We have studied the problem quite thoroughly in the time remaining. There is no other solution."

Kirk desperately wished he could read the expressions on the face of the speaker.

"The others are dead. Only I am left, to give warning. If you are understanding this message, comprehend that you are protected in this room only for the moment. The Thing . . . grows ever stronger . . . it wants . . ."

A spectacular flare of green phosphorescence erupted from the region of the doorway. The voice of the speaking alien was drowned out by a violent, hysterical flow of pure energy. Then the three segments of the door exploded inward as though struck by a small meteor.

The shock threw Dr. McCoy and Scott off the dais. Kirk and Spock were knocked down, but managed to hold onto the control chair and console. Fortunately, the splinters of flying metal from the ruined door somehow missed everyone.

The great curved mirror-screen began to vibrate, shiver as tremendous unrestrained power was played through it. A wash of stunning olivine boomed across the surface, absorbing the milky opalescence, drowning out all other colors. There was a deep rumbling.

The polished surface started to quiver at fantastic speed, then to flow. A crackling sound followed, then another, and another as shards of mirror material broke free, fell from the screen to the floor. Another powerful explosion tore the remainder of the wonderful device into tiny pieces of shining metal and blew a deep hole in the structure of the interior pod wall.

Clinging desperately to the unsteady, rocking console, Kirk and Spock watched as even the smallest fragment of mirror-screen was enveloped in soft green light. Each bit was then melted into a tiny, shapeless blob of hot metal.

At that point the command chair and console began to glow faintly green. Spock noticed it just in time.

"Off, Captain!"

Kirk was already jumping clear. Seconds later the temporary control center began to glow white-hot beneath enveloping green mists, then to run and drip like hot butter.

All around the great chamber, the other previously untouched mechanisms and devices started to show the now deadly green fire.

Kirk had a supportive arm around a dazed but otherwise unhurt Scott. Spock aided McCoy, who likewise had only been stunned.

"Out of here!" Kirk shouted into space. "Hurry!" Several pseudopods of translucent green started to advance towards them from various melting panels.

The men froze. Glaring light played suddenly over their forms. They dissolved, became four small shapeless masses of colored particles.

". . . Located them right after you pinned down the area of that last explosion, Mr. Sulu," said Transporter Chief Kyle into the intercom. His hands were smoothly operating the transporter controls as he spoke.

"Locked on and beaming them aboard," he finished.

"Good work, Chief." Uhura's voice echoed back over the grid from the distant bridge. "I thought we'd lost them when we were first cut off. And then when the pod they entered started to blow . . ."

Kyle looked up into the transporter alcove, saw flashing pillars beginning to take on solid, familiar outlines.

"Piece of cake, ma'm. They're coming through now."

The gleaming cylinders continued to build and take bipedal form. Kyle studied his dials and indicators intently, moved the levers down the final notch.

Kirk was in the foremost transporter disk. He blinked, took in the transporter room at a glance, and grinned in relief at Kyle. His expression changed fast when he noticed the chief's face. Kyle wore the strangest expression, of shock, perhaps. He was staring and pointing at Kirk—no, not at him, behind him.

"Chief," he began, "what's the—"

"Captain!" Kyle finally managed to gasp out, gesturing. "Something beamed aboard with you!" Kirk whirled, looked behind him. So did Spock and Scott and McCoy.

The fifth disk was occupied . . . by a glowing and pulsing shapeless green mass.

"Transport it back out!" In an instant Kirk was dashing for the transporter console where the chief stood frozen. He dove for the activating switch. He'd think about saving Spock and McCoy and Scott later.

Too late.

The entire transporter room was suddenly drenched in light the color of deep rain forests, in diffused energy that tingled and sent waves of terror over every man present. Then the walls seemed to suck up the light like a sponge.

Kirk recovered, his hand precious centimeters short of the activating lever. Might as well have been parsecs. Standing slowly he looked around and saw that Spock and the others were staring at the walls. Then he noticed it also. The walls of the transporter chamber were now radiating a faint, greenish glow.

At the same instant a roar of sound burst from the

ship's speakers. A bizarre, untranslatable, somehow triumphant cry. It was repeated, once.

In space, the *Enterprise*—infinitely tiny compared to the giant alien starship—suddenly flared with a halo of pale green. Then the seething mist thinned as the ship's hull seemed to reabsorb the color into itself.

Kirk let out his breath slowly, trying to regularize his metabolism.

"Mr. Scott, are you all right?" The engineer was staring blankly at the no longer friendly walls. His gaze held hints of panic.

"MR. SCOTT!"

The engineer shook at the verbal blast, but it was what was needed. He drew himself up, holding his right shoulder with his free arm.

"Yes, Captain. This is just a bruise. But what . . . ?"

"Bones?"

McCoy rose slowly from his kneeling position on the platform, brushed at his lower back and grimaced, then nodded.

"I'll be all right, Jim."

Two unrelenting forces flowed through the *Enterprise* then. A green something that had lived at least three hundred million years ago now permeated the entire ship, and a holocaust of thought racing through the mind of her captain, who had lived somewhat less.

# IV

Kirk, Spock, and Scott moved toward the bridge. Despite his continuing curiosity, McCoy had left them at another level. His job was elsewhere now.

To their credit, the crew on the bridge had remained reasonably calm. Less highly trained personnel might have done something drastic. The three returning officers took up their regular stations. A glance served to pass command back from Uhura to Kirk. They had no time to waste on formalities.

Reports were starting to filter onto the bridge from the rest of the ship as different sections responded to Kirk's request for status reports. His initial nervousnesss relaxed, but did not disappear, as section after section reported neither damage nor loss of life—no harm done by the strange discharge of green energy.

Or whatever it was.

He sighed as Uhura relayed the report he most wanted to hear.

"Sick Bay reports, sir. Dr. McCoy on alert—no injuries."

"No damage to engines or hull structure, Captain," came Scott's report a moment later.

So the *Enterprise* was still healthy, organically and inorganically. That was something, at least. They'd been given some time.

But how much?

"Automatic bridge defense system activated and operating, Captain." This from Spock.

Kirk spared an idle checking glance up and behind. A small metal globe, looking rather like a child's toy ball studded with tiny pipes now protruded downward from a small hatch in the ceiling. A tiny red light on its side winked on, showing that the automatic phaser mechanism was powered up and ready to deal with any intruder.

Kirk had seen the last-gasp defenses of the enormous alien ship fail in an attempt to halt the forays of the green light. He didn't pin much faith on the powerful phaser.

He nodded in acknowledgment and turned to study the main viewscreen. The now familiar shape of the ancient traveler, in reduced perspective, still floated against the vast blackness of dead sun, empty space. He thought a moment, then activated the chair comm unit, leaning slightly forward to project clearly.

"Uhura, give me all intership speakers. Open channel."

"Channels open, Captain."

"All sections are to remain on full alert until further notice. Section reports from Sick Bay indicate your companions are all unharmed. Engineering reports no damage to the ship. Nevertheless you will remain on full alert until told otherwise. All personnel will wear . . ." He caught himself. He'd almost said "will wear sidearms."

What would they shoot at—green light?

"All personnel will wear clothes." Sulu and Scott tried to stifle laughs, failed. McCoy would have approved. He tried to think of something brilliant to conclude with, failed as usual. "Everybody do your job . . . be ready for developments . . . and relax. Further orders and information will be forthcoming."

He switched off the communicator and found that everyone was watching him expectantly.

"So—we're in great shape, aren't we? But whatever was on that ship—" and he indicated the floating alien starship, "used our transporter beam to come aboard when it was good and ready. I don't think there's any question but that it allowed the alien's defense system to jam our communicators, the transporter, and our phasers until it was prepared to board the *Enterprise* itself."

"This in itself says that it has some limitations, Captain," suggested Spock. "If it was forced to rely on our transporter, then it seems certain it cannot move freely through space."

"That's true. We may have occasion to hope it has other limitations, Spock."

"That alien commander, sir," said Scott slowly, choosing his words with care. "At least, I assume it was the commander. His message confirmed that they had to destroy themselves. Why?"

Kirk didn't reply. He sat and stared closely at his left foot. It was as good a subject to focus concentration on as anything else. Staring at Uhura would be more pleasant, but would have the opposite effect. Despite his concentration he was aware that everyone was still watching him, waiting. As usual, they expected him to get them out of this. It was so goddamn unfair!

Kirk's opinion was not unique in the thoughts of captains.

When he finally spoke, the words came slow but clear.

"Until we learn more about this creature, Scotty, perhaps we should be prepared to do the same." He paused, but Scott wasn't going to help him out on this one. He'd have to say the words himself.

"Take two of your men and arm the self-destruct mechanism in the engine core."

"Sir?"

"You heard, Mr. Scott. Carry out your orders."

Scott came erect, snapped off a sharp salute.

"Aye, sir!"

An interval of solemn, respectful silence followed as the chief engineer left the bridge. He could have delegated the task to his assistants, but that was not Montgomery Scott's way.

"Mr. Spock, any change in the *Enterprise*'s readings? Anything to indicate what this creature may be up to?"

"Nothing obvious or immediate, Captain. We are registering a slightly higher than normal magnetic flux. It's not dangerous—not as it reads now. However, if it should go higher . . . and the level isn't constant. It appears to be fluctuating irregularly. There is some slight pattern, some half rhythm to these pulsations, but nothing recognizable enough to . . ."

Kirk barely heard the rest. "Like the beating of a heart," he muttered, half to himself.

A light blinked on suddenly on Uhura's board. No one turned immediately to watch her. At the moment, private thoughts were of greater importance.

"Bridge here." She paused, listening. Her life-support aura formed a lemon-colored nimbus around her, contrasting sharply with the red uniform of a communications officer.

"*What?*" The loud exclamation brought Kirk around. "Thank you, Lieutenant." She swiveled to face the Captain. Her voice was grim.

"Sir, decks five and six report shutdown of all life-support systems." An anticipatory shudder seemed to run through the bridge. "They'd just gone over to life-support belts—there was barely enough time." She paused.

"If you hadn't given the order for full alert, sir . . ." She left the obvious unsaid.

"What about manual override?" Uhura shook her head.

"According to the officers in charge, manual overrides have failed to respond, and—"

The raucous blare of the general alarm drowned out her concluding statements and all other sounds on the bridge. Kirk spoke angrily.

"Cut that, Mr. Sulu."

Flashing lights and siren died quickly. He shifted in his chair. "Mr. Spock!"

"Still checking, Captain," came the science officer's calm, reassuring tones. "Here it is—trouble in the engineering core, Captain."

"Damn. Any injuries?"

"I do not know, Captain. Apparently the alarm was sounded, but no one remained at the engineering communicator to supply answers to queries."

Kirk shook his head in disbelief. Didn't *anyone* remember his training?

"Bridge to Sick Bay," he began, speaking into the communicator he'd been pounding for the last ten minutes. "Bones, get down to Engineering Central, on the double. No, I don't know what it is, but that's where the general alarm was sounded." Another call switch down.

"Life-Support Central . . . LIFE-SUPPORT!"

"Life Support here . . . Lt. Crandall, sir."

"Get on those dead systems on decks five and six, Lieutenant. Draw any additional personnel you need from other sections, but get on them!" If the hard-pressed Crandall desired to reply, she didn't get the chance. Kirk was already heading for the elevator with Spock close behind.

The lights in the elevators ticking off the different decks seemed to pass with maddening slowness.

"What now, Spock?" he muttered tightly.

"I cannot say, Captain—but I venture to guess that the problems in engineering, as well as in life-support, are due

to the conscious intervention of the creature that managed
to beam aboard with us."

"Yes, of course—but what's it doing, Spock? Conscious, perhaps, but is it random or guided consciousness
that's at work here? What's its purpose? Or does it have
one?"

"Xenopsychology is not one of my specialties, Captain.
At this stage we can only be certain that its intentions are
both destructive and combative in nature—whether
guided by intelligence we cannot yet say for sure, though
its actions would tend to suppport such a hypothesis."

The light to the engineering core blinked solid green,
inviting egress.

Kirk smiled sourly. "Bones was right about your facility
for understatement. 'Combative!' " They stepped out.

This was the real heart of the *Enterprise,* just as the
bridge was her "brain." Awesome energies worked quietly
here, tremendous force was channeled, contained, kept
domesticated. It was an awkward place to have trouble.

A number of engineers, technicians, and a few security
personnel were clustered at the far end of the chamber.
They shifted, moving wordlessly aside as Kirk and Spock
approached. Dr. McCoy was already there, kneeling next
to a partly opened hatchway.

The hatch leading to the maintainance tube that in turn
led out to the central core was closed nearly all the way.
Nearly, because chief engineer Scott was holding it open.
He was pinned securely between the enormous weight of
the power-activated hatch cover and the floor. It pressed
against his waist, and the lime-yellow glow of his life-support force-field flared redly at the point of contact.

Another few steps and Kirk was able to kneel next to
the trapped engineer. Scott looked up at him and smiled
grimly. He was in no real pain, as yet. Kirk touched the
smooth metal of the hatch cover—its engaged closing
mechanism now humming softly, irregularly—and felt as
helpless as it was possible for a starship captain to feel.

Spock had detached himself from the group and had
moved immediately to the nearby control panel. Now he
was conferring intently with the assistant engineer in
charge. The assistant was a thin young man with a wisp of

blond mustache and an earnest expression. Just now he was perspiring heavily.

Meanwhile Kirk managed to dredge up a smile, somehow. It wasn't much, but Scott apparently appreciated it. He smiled back.

"How are you doing, Scotty?" Kirk finally said to break the silence.

"I'm all right, sir." Kirk reflected on how adversity made liars of all men. Scott's voice was tinged with nervousness, if not pain. "There's a good side to everything, I suppose. If the general alarm hadn't been given, I wouldn't have been wearing my life-support belt. And if the belt hadn't been activated, well——" he grinned faintly, "there'd be two of me now."

"The force-field of his belt won't hold against that kind of constant pressure for long, Jim," noted McCoy softly. Kirk, who was about to admonish McCoy for mentioning it so loudly, reflected that if anyone knew the capabilities and limitations of the belt fields, it was Scott.

"I know that, Bones." He looked over toward the control panel. "Override system, Mr. Spock. Open the core hatch."

Scott shook his head slowly.

"It's no good, Captain. The mechanism's been frozen in the close mode. We tried everything."

Spock looked over from his position at the controls.

"Engineer Scott is correct, sir. Something has jammed all circuits. Very effectively, too."

Think . . . think . . . ! Kirk studied the massive hatch cover closely, sought ideas in the intermittent hum of the servomotor.

"Scotty, is there a manual device for handling this baby?"

"No, sir. Its designers never envisioned a situation where it might be necessary to move such a heavy, vital piece of machinery by hand. Security has something to do with it, too. Anyhow, the last command it received was to close. Only the computer can tell it otherwise, sir, and it's blocked, as Mr. Spock says. Nothin' mere muscles can do is goin' to force it backwards against that command."

As he finished, a desperately bright flare of red came

from the place where the cover rested against his force-field and waist. He squirmed uncomfortably. The brighter flare was the belt's way of warning its wearer that they were approaching a critical point.

"Gettin' a little weak, sir," he said unnecessarily.

Kirk spun and glared at the watching engineers and technicians. "Well, what are you all mooning at? The *Enterprise* can survive without one hatch cover. We'll have to. Maybe we can jury-rig an emergency radiation shield. Get those cutter beams out, Move!"

"Yes, sir!" replied one of the mesmerized engineers. Then they all seemed to be moving at once, like an army of toy soldiers.

Kirk studied his trapped chief engineer, and Scott smiled reassuringly back at him. Which was damned odd. It ought to be the other way around, he reflected. But that was the kind of person Scott was—always worried about others first. Quiet, more reserved than Spock in some ways, less ebullient than McCoy, Kirk tried to think of some way to make small talk, but nothing that came to mind seemed in any way appropriate.

Despite the fact that starship captains were not permitted the option of being maudlin, for the moment, at least, the alien invader was completely forgotten.

Two of the engineers finally returned and began setting up a complicated arrangement of spools and spheres and silicon spirals on a flexible tripod. Kirk backed away. One of the engineers gave a ready signal. Scott bent his head down to his chest and turned away as much as he could, covering his face with his arms. Both engineers wore thick goggles.

Kirk put his own hands over his eyes to shield himself. There was a soft click. An incredibly brilliant, seemingly solid line of violent, violet light lanced out from the tip of the heavy-duty cutter. It touched one of the thick hinges at the back of the hatch cover.

Immediately the hinge began to glow a deep red, shading rapidly to white. A moment more and the metal began to flow like gray milk. The hissing of the melting metal was the only sound in the engineering section.

What seemed like ages later there was a dull snap, and the hinge was cut through. The engineers instantly switched off the cutter. Now pressing shut with only a single activated hinge, the hatch cover was canted at a definite awkward angle. Scott was just able to struggle free, carefully avoiding the still white-hot area where the one hinge had been melted away.

Kirk gave him a hand up. The chief was unhurt, only badly shaken.

"Be nice to be able to be in two places at the same time, sir," he commented, "but I don't fancy managin' it in quite this way. In the final reckoning it's a mite too divisible."

Sulu's voice sounded over the open intercom before Kirk could reply.

"Bridge to Captain Kirk."

He moved to stand near the pickup. "What is it, Sulu?"

"Sir, something's taken over the ship's phaser banks! They're locking on the alien starship."

Now what? He dismissed the engineers and security men to their normal duties, then moved to the small wall-screen set close by the communicator. A quick touch and once more they were treated to a view of the magnificent, ancient vessel.

Suddenly, two thick beams of destroying energy licked out. They struck the alien, struck again. Huge sections of metallic lacework were blasted apart. Archwork and shattered pods disappeared as bolt after bolt of phaser energy tore at the helpless derelict. Bits and pieces vanished in a maelstrom of organized destruction.

Torn free and impelled by the force of the phasers' power, segments of the ship began to spin end over end. They dropped out of ages-old orbit, falling into the crushing gravity-well of the waiting dead sun. Kirk's comment came in a whisper.

"The creature has no respect for beauty, either."

"Or history, Captain," Spock added, equally shocked by the invader's actions. "All that knowledge . . . all those potential discoveries—lost forever."

"Perhaps even more, Mr. Spock."

Sulu showed obvious relief when the others reappeared on the bridge. He'd watched the dissolution of the alien vessel and experienced an unusual feeling of impotence as the phaser banks, usually under his control, failed to respond to repeated attempts to halt firing.

Kirk listened to his helmsman's comments as he resumed his command position.

"Phaser banks were off, Captain. They activated themselves. I tried, sir," he half-pleaded, "but—"

"Override systems refused to respond?"

"Yes, sir. How did you know, sir?"

"The same thing just happened in engineering, Mr. Sulu," informed Spock. "The same thing which has affected the life-support systems on decks five and six. About all that can be said in favor of our visitor is that it is not capricious. It is clearly about some private plan of its own. One which we seem quite unable to alter."

"If we only knew what it wants!" Kirk muttered through clenched teeth. The familiar hiss of the elevator doors operating sounded. He turned to see Scott and Dr. McCoy appear.

"No internal damage, Jim," said McCoy, nodding in the chief engineer's direction. "He's fine."

Scott's expression, however, was less encouraging.

"Let's have it, Scotty. Nothing you can say could really upset me any further—not now."

"Sir, we cannot get into the core. All exits are sealed. And that means . . ."

"That you can't arm the *Enterprise*'s self-destruct mechanism. What about cutter beams? They still seem to work. Can't you cut your way . . . ?" He paused. Scott was shaking his head slowly.

"They might've worked a little while ago, sir. They're drained of all energy now. Apparently this creature has to sense something in operation before it can drain that something of power, or counter its command source. I don't pretend to understand how the creature does it, but there isn't a cutting or weldin' or seaming tool in the whole engineering section putting out enough juice to rearrange a loaf of stale bread."

"Captain—" Kirk turned his gaze to Uhura.

"What new good news do you have now, Lieutenant?"

"Cargo holds three, four, and five report shutdown of life-support systems. They've gone to belt-support."

"Terrific—that's just marvelous!" He spared a glance for the emergency telltales located at Scott's station. Spotted among the normal greens and blues were an uncomfortably large number of flashing reds. Even one of the galley lights was winking crimson.

"What the hell would the thing want in the galley?"

"Sir?" asked Spock, failing to sense the irony in Kirk's voice.

"Power is now out on all but key levels, Captain," informed Scott. "I'm getting a strong magnetic flux reading on all out decks."

"Captain!" Uhura shouted. She was staring in disbelief at her instruments. "Something's going through every computer bank on board, every microspool, every tape, every storage bin—and fast!"

Spock had backed slightly away from his station, watching while his dials and checkouts gave back impossible readings. Sulu's hands hovered hesitantly over his own console. The telltales of all the bridge computer systems—navigation, library, communications, engineering—were alive with myriad flashing, sparkling lights. All indications were that information was being processed through them simultaneously at an unbelievable rate.

Then the double-red local emergency lights went on, and the bridge alarm howled. They had very little autonomy left—or time. If Kirk was going to do anything he'd have to do it now. His mind raced. One last computer was as yet uncontrolled, unread, by the invader—a delicate marvel that could also process information with more insight, if not more speed, than all the onboard ship computers put together.

"Spock," he murmured finally, "can you rig a temporary, low-frequency shield, like the one we found on the alien ship, for our own navigation console?"

Spock hesitated briefly. "It would have to be a very small field, Captain."

"That's all right, Mr. Spock. Just the navigation console. I don't expect you to be able to whip up a convenient, invader-proof, bridge defense system in a couple of minutes. We're short on time."

That was enough for Spock. He bent over the navigation console and started to work smoothly, efficiently, among the instruments. Occasionally he asked Sulu for help and advice on this or that particular piece of circuitry or had him depress this or the other switch at a certain time.

Meanwhile, the force-fields of both men flared and gleamed bright as Spock played with local but powerful energies. The resulting radiance and field interaction gave each man a satanic silhouette.

Scott was bursting to complain about the lack of adequate safety precautions for such work, but he managed to contain himself. They had no time to be careful anymore.

After an interval of minutes that seemed like years, Spock stood and walked back to his station. Scott eyed the critical meters on his board and let out a sigh of relief.

"It's activated and in operation, Captain—but only for an area three meters square."

"How's the flux reading there now?" Kirk asked. Spock took his tricorder off a rack and moved back to stand close by the shielded section of console. He played the compact instrument over the affected section.

"Negative reading, Captain. The shielded area is completely normal." He moved the tricorder randomly over other sections of the helm. "Especially now, compared to what the rest of the panel reads. Readings here are rising rapidly."

McCoy took a couple of steps forward and stared at the slightly lime-yellow section of shielded console in disbelief.

"Jim, you don't think this is going to help? Whatever this monster is, it's survived eons alone in a dead, empty hulk. All it has to do here is outlast us and take over."

Kirk's reply was rich with a certain morbid satisfaction.

"No, Bones. It is obviously trapped here by the gravitational power of the negative star-mass. We have already ascertained that it cannot travel freely in open space. Therefore it doubly needs a starship—this starship—to break free. And it must also need a crew to man it. Otherwise it would have left here long ago in the alien vessel we explored. Because—"

Further elaboration was cut off as the room suddenly was bathed in shades of color as brilliant as cut emerald. Something . . . spoke—using the computer speakers. The phrasing was oddly rushed, childishly impatient. But it was not the impatience of uncertainty, for no voice was more self-assured, more fully confident than this.

This is what it said.

"YOU ARE CORRECT, CAPTAIN JAMES T. KIRK! I POSSESS A GREAT MANY ABILITIES. BUT THE ABILITY TO BREAK FREE OF THE PULL OF THIS GRAVITY-WELL IS NOT ONE OF THEM. SO I DID . . . I DO . . . NEED A STARSHIP. NOW I HAVE ONE."

The voice rose to a shrill, almost hysterical scream.

"A BODY . . . TO HAVE A BODY . . . TO HAVE FORM . . . SOLID, SENSUOUS, AGAIN! SO LONG . . . SO TERRIBLY LONG!"

The voice ended abruptly. The flashing lights on the computer telltales suddenly died. Only the normal blink of standard activity now registered. If anything, the panels were even quieter than usual.

Spock ventured back to his library station and tried the controls. They worked normally. Only their readings and the information they now provided were abnormal. He studied them a moment, then looked back at Kirk.

"It has absorbed the computer banks, Captain. All of them. Language was naturally but one small section of the total information it gleaned."

Kirk eyed the walls thoughtfully, trying to penetrate to the heart of the softly ominous green glow that pulsed there.

"All the information in all the worlds of the Federation won't give it what it needs, Spock. A manipulative digit. In going through your library, I'm sure it discovered that we carry no manipulative robots on board that it could control."

If the captain expected that statement to provoke the creature, he failed. The alien seemed to have only a single tone of voice. One continuous flow of nervous emotion. The voice was a mirror image of its actions—violent and quick. It ignored the mild sarcasm, if indeed it was sensible to such subtleties, and spoke with single-minded purpose.

"YOU WILL NOW REMOVE THE STATIC SHIELD FROM THE NAVIGATION CONSOLE, CAPTAIN JAMES T. KIRK."

Kirk considered his reply carefully. It might still be posssible to reason with this thing.

"You've shut down life-support systems and threatened the lives of my crew. I'll remove the static shield if you restore those systems first."

As he half-expected, even that modest request was denied. No, not even denied. It was ignored, treated as unworthy of comment. For this being, nothing existed outside of self.

"ALL NONESSENTIAL SYSTEMS HAVE BEEN EXTINGUISHED IN THE INTERESTS OF SIMPLIFYING CONTROL. OBEY ME!"

That made his decision simpler, if not more pleasant.

"And if I refuse?"

A phaser beam darted out of nowhere as Kirk rose in the command chair. No, it issued from ... the automatic bridge defense system! The beam impacted on his forcefield squarely and knocked him stumbling into a bulkhead.

"OBEY ME!" the alien thundered from all speakers.

Kirk tried to dodge out of the phaser's line of fire and searched frantically for cover. But he couldn't dodge the beam of the phaser anymore than one could escape sun in a desert. As for finding cover, the automatic defense system was very thorough. It had been carefully designed to permit a hostile intruder *no* cover.

The beam cut off for seconds, shot out again, and slammed him against a wall. It pinned him there like some shriveled, colorful insect. His force-field flared pink, then red, turning slowly to a deep crimson. Beads of sweat began to form on his forehead. Though it hadn't broken through, the intense concentration of heat was starting to hurt like blazes. He felt himself weakening, slumped against the wall.

"Captain!"

Spock ran toward him, stopped. The beam left Kirk for

a split second, affording him little relief. It moved to Spock. But when the science officer remained frozen in place, it swung back to batter again at Kirk's shield.

Spock took a heavy, metal-spined reference manual from a shelf and stepped quickly toward the bridge defense module. As he threw, the phaser beam looped around and struck at his ankles. The thrown book fell far short, bounced over the command chair. Moving higher the powerful beam shoved Spock back against the base of the library computer. Then it shifted slightly and he was washed down the floor along the wall like a leaf in the grip of a powerful hose.

It finally pinned him upright against a far bulkhead, holding him there until his force-field also flared pink, red, and crimson.

Kirk put a hand to his singed chest and rolled over slowly. He staggered to his feet. The first thing he saw was Spock, pinned up against the wall. Swaying, he took a step toward the science officer. It was the shock of the near-fatal phaser assault that had affected him, more than any actual physical damage. He knew what an uncontrolled phaser of even mild strength could do to something as fragile as a human body.

At that moment there was a deep red flare, almost black, from Spock's life-support belt. Then his force-field was gone, overloaded by the concentration of energy from the phaser. Immediately the beam stepped down to low power. It continued to focus on the center of Spock's chest. Kirk could have continued to advance, but now dared not.

From somewhere in the depths of the ship, from all around them, the implacable alien consciousness spoke.

"OBEY ME!"

It was Kirk's turn to scream.

"You'll hurt him!"

"REMOVE THE STATIC SHIELD FROM THE DRIVE CONTROLS AND NAVIGATION PANEL! DO IT NOW!"

No hint of compassion—not even a mention of Spock. There was absolutely no doubt in Kirk's mind that the creature would kill Spock slowly, without thought.

The subject lying under that threat still had his voice, if not his mobility.

"No, Captain!"

The phaser beam intensified ever so lightly. No cry of pain escaped Spock's lips, but he writhed. A tensing in the knuckles showed what he was feeling. Inwardly, Kirk slumped.

"I will obey. Let him go."

As quickly as that, the phaser beam was gone. Spock stood leaning against the wall for a moment longer. Then his legs gave way under him and he collapsed to the floor. Kirk took a step in his direction, but that damnable, all-seeing voice interrupted again, bellowing.

"NOW! IGNORE THE FALLEN BIPED AND PROCEED WITH THE FIELD REMOVAL!"

He turned and started reluctantly to the helm-navigation console. McCoy moved to Spock's side. There was a small but neat hole in the center of the science officer's shirt. McCoy dug out a tiny spray vial and began to work on the injury.

Kirk thought furiously. It was the end of everything—unless . . .

He looked down at his chest, where he'd been lightly burned . . . lower, to his stomach. His hand slipped slowly ever so slowly, down to his life-support belt.

"It's too fast for us, Doctor," Kirk said quickly. "So don't try deactivating the defense module with one of your sprays." McCoy looked up, puzzled.

Had the alien learned enough to read a human expression?

It had not. McCoy's response was to look at Kirk. In doing so he automatically brought the spray vial away from Spock, and up. The phaser shifted to cover McCoy and the almost awake Spock.

In that brief, unguarded instant Kirk whipped free his life-support belt with one hand, hit a switch on the console with the other, and dropped the activated belt across a certain unshielded section of it. He jumped clear as the panel erupted in sparks and fiery flashes.

He'd been gambling that the creature wouldn't turn off

the bridge life-support systems and risk killing them all. He was right.

But the phaser beam swung to burn an opening in the floor. Desperately he rolled to get away from it. It eventually caught up with him at the other end of the helm console. Stopping, the beam focused just a few centimeters to one side of his head. He could feel the deadly heat on his cheek. The beam had been raised to killing force.

## V

"REPAIR THE WARP-DRIVE CONTROLS! OBEY ME!"

The now maddened voice had risen to a tremulous shriek.

Kirk got to his feet slowly, cautiously, making sure he made no rapid gestures that might be misinterpreted by the trigger-happy alien. As he rose the beam stayed centered parallel to his skull. He walked to the command chair.

"Mr. Scott."

"Yes, sir?"

"The warp-drive controls have burned out. Commence repairs immediately. Install the auxiliary bypass system."

If Scott suspected anything, he gave no sign.

"Aye, Captain." He looked around, his gaze coming to rest on the somnolent bridge defense mechanism. It was as good a point to direct his voice to as any.

"I'll need some cuttin' and repairin' tools." He pointed to a nearby locker. "I can get what I need in there—if you'll allow them to energize."

"YES, YES!" came the anxious voice. "BUT MAKE NO

WRONG MOTIONS. I HAVE THE ENTIRE WARP-DRIVE
AUXILIARY BYPASS SYSTEM AND REPAIR PROCEDURE FROM
YOUR OWN COMPUTER RECORDS. HURRY!"

"Do as it says, Mr. Scott."

"Aye, Captain," Scott replied, keeping a determined
pokerface. Not that he knew what Kirk had in mind, but
he suspected the captain was up to *something*. And it was
up to him to give Kirk as much time as posssible to
prepare for it.

He walked slowly to the locker, at the same time being
careful not to move unnaturally and thus make the creature suspicious. There was a nervous moment as he energized the precision microwelder. Small as it was, it could
still easily burn a hole even in a bridge defense module—
if given the time.

However, the alien apparently felt secure in its control.
It permitted him the necessary small tool. He walked to
the fused section of helm, examined it, and shook his head
like a doctor clucking over a sick patient.

Then he moved to the back of the bridge, near Uhura's
station, and a small wall panel that needed to be removed.
Controls and switching points were revealed within. There
were also several long coils of fine cable.

As he brought the activated welder close and began to
make the necessary connections, the voice again reverber-
ated around the bridge.

"ANY ATTEMPT TO SABOTAGE THE AUXILIARY WARP-
DRIVE CONTROLS, CHIEF ENGINEER MONTGOMERY SCOTT,
WILL RESULT IN IMMEDIATE DESTRUCTION OF ALL OTHER
BRIDGE PERSONNEL. I WOULD RATHER NOT RESORT TO
THE USE OF INFERIOR, SECONDARY PERSONNEL TO CARRY
OUT MY COMMANDS—BUT I WILL NOT HESITATE!"

"I'll be sure to try and keep that in mind," Scott mumbled, concentrating on the delicate work at hand.

Spock was on his feet again. He touched his chest once,
looked at McCoy.

"A fine, professional job, Doctor. Fortunately, your
medicine is more effective than your jokes." For once,
McCoy didn't feel up to a reply.

The science officer walked over to stand next to Kirk.
Both faced casually away from the bridge defense system's

video pickup. Apparently the creature's abilities did not also include mind reading. It had divined nothing of Kirk's series of delaying actions beyond their immediate practical effects.

The defense sphere's sound pickups were not designed to detect whispering. It was primarily a visual device. Normal ship noises would have drowned out soft talk and only confused an efficient mechanism. So the two men felt reasonably secure in conversing.

"Let's have it all, Spock. You've had enough experience with this creature's actions to have formed some solid opinions about it, at least. What are we dealing with?"

Spock rubbed his chest again. "Beyond its undeniable belligerence, Captain, we know nothing about its mental composition. We can theorize more thoroughly about its physical makeup.

"It seems to be some form of pure energy organism, without much actual mass, and it is essentially electromagnetic in nature. At the same time, it appears capable of a strong parasitic relationship with a solid host body. A starship could provide such a body, it seems.

"It appears to utilize the electronic network of the *Enterprise* the way a man or Vulcan uses the nervous system of his body. It has, in effect, become the *Enterprise*. We, on the other hand, are only marginally beneficial organisms in its structure, like the white corpuscles in human blood. That is, some of us are. Apparently it regards most of the crew as unwelcome growths—germs—simply to be disposed of as rapidly and with as little effort as possible.

"And, Captain, the computer library still operates. It has indicated that the flux readings are growing in strength. The longer this being has to adjust to its new body, the stronger and more secure it grows."

Kirk dropped his voice even lower. If the alien could somehow pick it up and understand it, then all was lost. But it had given no sign of being able to so far. And devilish subtlety did not seem to be one of its characteristics. They had no choice but to try. Spock was looking at him expectantly and Kirk remembered that he couldn't read minds, either.

"The slingshot effect, to throw us free of this gravity

and out of orbit—can you do the necessary math in your mind, Spock? I've got reasons for not using the navigation computer."

Spock nodded. "I see. Yes, the alien would know. I believe I can, Captain. Soon I will have to aid Mr. Scott, but my mind and hands can operate on different projects at the same time."

Kirk turned and raised his voice as he addressed the rotating sphere of the defense mechanism.

"The chief engineer will need assistance from my first officer to complete repairs. Is this permitted?"

Circuits continued to open and close. Human diaphragms operated somewhat slower. Otherwise there was little motion on the bridge. Spock strode slowly, cautiously, to where Scott was working. Kirk kept a wary eye on the dormant phaser, but no punishment, no warning was forthcoming.

"I guess it is," he murmured.

"WHEN REPAIRS ARE COMPLETED," came the voice suddenly and, as usual, without any warning, "YOU WILL LEAVE THIS ORBIT AND PLOT A COURSE THIRTY-SIX POINT THREE TWO ONE FROM OUR PRESENT LOCATION."

Sulu spoke up.

"That's the heart of the galaxy, Captain!"

"Set the course, Mr. Sulu."

Sulu looked back at him incredulously and made no move to obey. Spock glanced over from his work and spoke.

"Captain, we've seen this creature separate itself into different parts. If it can divide and grow, it could take over every starship we meet. It could control entire computer centers—perhaps whole planets."

"I am aware of that, Mr. Spock. But we have," and he looked downcast, "no choice, I'm afraid."

"COMPLETE REPAIRS!" screamed the voice. "OBEY ME!"

"Set the course, Mr. Sulu! That's an order."

"Yes, sir." Sulu's reply held a hint of bitterness.

Scott and Spock unwound two small cables from the recess in the wall and ran them along the deck to the burned-out navigation console. Working with the microwelder and Spock's assistance, Scott proceeded to install a small metal box to one side of the melted panel.

The box's face contained a basic, simplified version of the ruined warp-drive controls. The engineer made a last connection, wiped his forehead with the back of a hand, and took a deep breath.

"Auxiliary controls ready to activate, Captain." Everyone on the bridge was staring at Kirk.

The Captain looked up at the sphere, hardly daring to breathe and yet forcing himself to maintain a normal tone of voice.

"The auxiliary controls can only be opened manually."

At that, the memory banks of Spock's computer-library station suddenly hummed into operation. No one needed to be told what was taking place. The creature was checking Kirk's statement against the operations manuals stored deep within the ship.

Eventually the lights at the computer station returned to normal. There was a short, screaming silence. Kirk willed himself not to sweat.

"THAT IS CORRECT. OPERATE THE MANUAL CONTROLS. OBEY!"

Kirk breathed an unseen sigh of thankfulness and offered prayer to all supernatural deities who looked after starship skippers. Then he nodded slowly to Scott.

The engineer moved back toward his own station. Kirk rose and walked calmly to the auxiliary control box. He placed his hands on the simplified device. It was only illusion, but the smooth metal controls and knobs felt hot.

"Control activated." He paused, started toward another set of switches. "Setting cour——" His hands moved in a blur.

The Enterprise's engines slammed into emergency drive. Not away, toward the beckoning mist of the Milky Way, but down, down and in, toward the devouring black maw below.

Sulu jerked in his seat as the dark bulk of the dead sun grew suddenly enormous in the main viewscreen. He spun to face Kirk.

"Captain, we're falling out of orbit! We're falling into the star!"

"APPLY FULL POWER—REVERSE ENGINES!" shrieked the disembodied alien. "OBEY ME, OBEY ME!"

The bridge defense phaser came on, swung around to touch Kirk's back. He jerked and hung grimly to the controls. He had no force-field to protect him now, with his life-support belt fused to the original controls.

Picking up speed with every microsecond, the *Enterprise* rushed toward the destroying gravity below. The phaser abruptly cut off—and Kirk cursed silently. The creature had guessed what he was trying to do. If it killed him while he was hanging onto the controls and failed to cut his hands free in time . . .

It tried something else, and for a few seconds Kirk was forced to fall away. The entire console section and even the deck around the manual control unit began to glow with heat. At the same time the walls of the bridge began to fluoresce an angry, pulsing green. The vivid color deepened and dimmed in indecipherable, distorted patterns. The voice of the alien rose to a terrible, frightened scream.

"NO, DECELERATE! DO NOT DESTROY THE SHIP! OBEY—OBEY—OBEY!"

Kirk had glanced down at his hands, then back at the glowing console. If the alien realized that at any second it could now safely kill him and induce another member of the crew to operate the controls . . .

He threw himself back on the metal box and its burning knobs and dials. There was a sizzling sound and the odor of burnt flesh filled the bridge. Uhura screamed. Tears streamed from Kirk's eyes, but his hands stayed frozen on the controls.

"Stand by to activate warp—drive!" he gasped. Spock instantly took the vacant assistant helmsman's place next to Sulu . . . in case.

"NO . . . DON'T!" came the terrified voice. The *Enterprise* dove toward the extinct solar furnace. It filled the viewscreen now, as complete a grave as any man could wish for. Its surface was alive with brilliant discharges of electricity.

The starship glowed all over with a soft green aura. This rapidly coalesced into a single, bright blob of beating, living light. On the bridge the green luminescence of the walls suddenly faded and seemed to sink into the metal. The phaser beam of the defense sphere abruptly cut off.

That was the first sign. Now for the final blow.

"Activate warp-drive!" Kirk managed to cough out. The white heat of the panel had vanished at the same time as the phaser beam, but the metal was still fearfully hot. If it was a last, desperate ruse by the creature to get him away from the controls, it failed.

"Activated, Captain," came Spock's prompt reply.

The ship shuddered briefly as the titanic warp-drive engines cut in. There was a last faint pulse of green radiance—then it was gone. A final, despairing cry, shrill and weak now, came from the speakers.

"PLEASE . . . DON'T!"

Suddenly the *Enterprise* seemed to leap toward the black sphere, toward the very horizon of the sun that was no more. It seemed impossible that it could miss that sucking, grasping target. It *must* strike, vanish in a blank flash of instant annihilation. The image of the starship wavered as it reached the critical point of that bottomless pit of gravity, seemed to flow like a liquid . . . and disappear.

An instant later the combination of emergency overdrive and the tremendous pull of the star had flung the *Enterprise* far beyond any threat—far beyond any clutch of its relentless tug.

For a few seconds the star wore a ring of incredible thinness. A tiny narrow band of soft green circled the black sphere, revealing a last, hopeless grab for a ship safely out of its reach. Forever out of its reach.

Then the green ring contracted, shrunk in on itself, to become a single bright, emerald blob of incandescent life—an amorphous mass of now harmless malevolence.

"You can let go now, Captain," said Spock gently.

"Let . . . go . . .?" Kirk mumbled. His eyes glazed. Spock reached over and gripped the captain's wrists. They pulled easily but that death grip was not so simply broken. Spock reached around more firmly and pulled, pulled again, hard. This time both hands came free of the controls.

Kirk slumped in Spock's arms, unconscious. The second-in-command of the *Enterprise* carried his captain over to the command chair. Sulu immediately put the helm on automatic and took over the warp-drive controls, his hands safely encased in a pair of thick protective gloves. He brought the *Enterprise* down from emergency to normal cruising speed.

McCoy had been waiting. Spock watched him at his work. When he spoke, his tone was as emotionless as ever—and as lucid, curious.

"Well, Doctor?" McCoy was already working with a second kind of spray, then rapidly applying some white cream to Kirk's hands—those blackened, terribly burned hands. The cream hardened instantly to an almost plastic consistency. He smiled just a little.

"I don't find any serious nerve damage, Mr. Spock. Nothing that won't repair itself. As for the skin, that's easy to regenerate. Oh, someone will have to feed him for a few days, but other than that . . ." He smiled wider. "He'll be as good as new."

Sulu, Uhura, and Scott all turned away—so that no one else could see how relieved they were. McCoy moved to the nearest intercom, which happened to be the one in the command chair, and thumbed the switch.

"Sick Bay? Doctor McCoy here. I want a medtable on the bridge, double-time."

Spock was watching Kirk. The captain's eyes fluttered as both anesthetic and stimulants took effect.

"Is it . . . it . . . gone?"

"Affirmative, Captain." At moments like this Spock almost wished he could smile—but only for the therapeutic effect it would have on Kirk, of course.

"It left the ship when it thought we would crash into the negative stellar mass. In the end it seems that the alien's instinct for self-preservation, even after all these millennia, was stronger than its analytic abilities. If it had gambled and stayed with us another few seconds it would still be with us. Now it is trapped back there once more.

"And now that we know it is there, we can enter its description, dangerous characteristics, and location with Starfleet, so that any other exploring vessels that visit this sector can give it a wide berth."

The elevator door dilated, and a pair of medical techs with a mobile medtable between them entered. Under McCoy's direction they lined it up parallel to the command chair. Both techs gave a little start when they saw that the patient-to-be was the captain, but McCoy reassured them.

"It's all right Darrell, Elayne—nothing too serious."

Kirk eyed the medtable and then shifted his gaze to the face of the good doctor.

"What's that for, Bones? I'm all right. You just said so yourself."

"I know, Jim. There's nothing wrong with you at all that a pair of new hands won't fix." He patted the table. "Be a good boy and climb aboard without forcing me to tranquilize you, hmmm? I will if I have to, you know."

"Okay, okay—! Don't threaten me, Bones."

"Threaten, Jim?" McCoy grinned.

With the help of the two techs and Spock, Kirk slid onto the table. The table was convoyed to the elevator.

"Wait a minute, Mr. Spock—Captain," Uhura broke in. McCoy froze the elevator open. Her brows drew together as she fiddled with her controls.

"We're still picking up emissions from the area of the dead star. It's growing faint as we move away, but . . . ah, there!" She did things with the amplifiers.

A tremulous, desperate voice filtered through the speaker. A familiar voice, made harmless now by increasing distance and hopelessness.

"DON'T LEAVE ME ALONE AGAIN! OH, PLEASE, PLEASE!"

No one on the bridge said anything. There was a crackle of static as a different source of distant energy from another star announced its own presence. Then a final, faint piping.

"SO LONELY . . . OH, DON'T GO! DON'T . . . DON . . ."

The voice vanished, swallowed down and digested by distance.

"It doesn't sound so dangerous now, does it, Mr. Spock?" Kirk whispered.

"The creature? No, Captain. Not now. But the danger behind it remains."

"If only the alien had tried to cooperate, to communicate instead of threaten . . ." He shook his head tiredly, beginning to feel the side effects of McCoy's ministrations as they rode down the elevator. He stared at the steady light set in its roof.

"What makes a thinking, intelligent being act in such a fashion?"

"Who knows, Captain? We know not where it comes from. And we do not even know what makes certain men or Vulcans act the way they do. The creature's instincts, in the final analysis, are not so incomprehensible—or even alien."

"Now you're acting unnecessarily rational, Spock."

"To me, Captain," Spock replied, "that is a contradiction in terms."

"You know," said Kirk abruptly, "I think I can feel my hands again. They're beginning to tingle slightly."

He felt a pressure on his upper right shoulder.

"What was that?" Turning his head slightly he saw that they were entering Sick Bay. "Bones, what have you done to me now?" McCoy smiled down at him reassuringly.

"You're coming out of shock, Jim. I just gave you a good dose of something to keep your mind off it. If I didn't, despite the local anesthetic, in a few minutes those hands would do more than just tingle slightly."

"Shock? What do you mean, shock? I'm not in shock, Spock." McCoy had to grin. "And nothing you slipped me, Bones, is going to make me go un . . ."

# PART II
# YESTERYEAR

(Adapted from a script by D. C. Fontana)

# VI

A world of silvery sky.

There seemed to be no oceans; but they were there, rolling and heaving under the shining clouds. There seemed to be no deserts; yet they existed, too. Dry, bone dry, and inhospitable, and old. There seemed to be no green forests or rolling hills. True, they were rare; but they too held a real existence.

There only seemed to be sky.

There was a peculiar atmospheric aura to this world—a kind of shimmer in the stratosphere that rippled and flowed with strange effects—other than merely meteorological.

Kirk finished his glass of reconstituted rombouton juice, prepared on a distant South Pacific isle on Earth itself, and studied the image on the viewscreen before him. He touched a button on the arm of the command chair and leaned over to direct his voice into the open grid.

"Captain's Log, stardate . . ." He burped, rather loudly, and looked around in mild embarrassment. Everyone on the bridge studiously avoided looking back at him. But at the helm, Sulu made a sound suspiciously like a stifled chuckle.

"You find our approach maneuvers amusing, Mr. Sulu?" Kirk was not in the best of moods. His newly regenerated skin on his hands itched something fierce.

"No, sir," deadpanned Sulu in return. He examined the readouts of the navigation computer most intently.

Satisfied that dignity had been maintained, Kirk hit the

switch once more. "Erase that last," he muttered, then began again.

"Captain's Log, Stardate 5373.4." He paused, formed his thoughts.

"After an unexpected delay of some substantial awkwardness . . ."

"What was that I once heard you say about my tendency to understate, Captain?" came Spock's quiet voice from the area of the library-computer console.

"Quiet, Mr. Spock. I'm recording. Or trying to." He hit the unlucky switch again, irritably. "Cancel that last.

"Captain's Log, stardate 5373.4 After an unexpected delay of some substantial awkwardness . . ." he glared around, but this time no one saw fit to interpose a comment, ". . . we resumed our original course and are now lying in orbit around the planet of the time vortex.

"Commander Spock and I will land to carry out basic research for the Institute of Galactic History, in conjunction with and in support of similar research to be conducted by historians Jan Grey, Loom Aleek-om, and Ted Erickson.

"Dr. Leonard McCoy will also accompany us, as . . ." He held the panic button down and looked back to where Dr. McCoy was standing, idly observing the view of the planet rotating lazily below. "How do you want to go into the record on this, Bones?"

"What?" McCoy dragged his attention away from the fascinating image of the time planet. "Oh, might as well play it linear, Jim. 'Interested onlooker' will do. I'm not hunting for academic credits."

"Attaboy, Bones. I thought you'd say something like that." Kirk let the pause switch up. ". . . as interested onlooker." Satisfied, he switched off the log and thumbed a communicator switch.

"Historians Grey, Aleek-om, and Erickson report to the transporter room, please. We are ready for descent." He flipped the communicator off and rose.

"Lieutenant Sulu?" The younger officer glanced up from the helm. "You're in command in my absence."

"Yes, sir," Sulu replied. He hesitated, then spoke quickly, earnestly. "I sure wish I was going down with you, sir. I've heard a great deal about the Guardian of Forever."

Spock and McCoy were waiting at the elevator, and Kirk moved to join them.

"It can be very interesting at times, Mr. Sulu—that's true. It can also be infernallly dull. Either way, you know the regulations. No one is permitted on the surface outside the reception station except authorized research personnel and Starfleet officers with the rank of Lt. Commander and above." He smiled.

"You'll be there in a couple of years, Lieutenant."

When they'd left, Sulu looked back at Uhura.

"Somehow, Uhura, I get the impression the captain's not terribly enthusiastic about this expedition."

Uhura replied while taking the opportunity—now that the commanding officers were absent—to touch up her makeup. "I suppose even the most exciting of pasts can grow dull with repetition. Seeing a famous person or witnessing an important historical event could be offset by bad smells and unsanitary plumbing.

"Besides, you can blame him for being a bit blasé after what we just went through with that—that *thing* on the fringe?" She whistled. "Substantial awkwardness . . . wow!"

The three historians were already waiting in the main transporter room when Kirk, Spock, and McCoy arrived. All appeared outwardly composed, but their faces betrayed the excitement they were feeling. Two had made the trip to the surface once before.

Their anticipation was understandable—history was their chosen profession. The discovery of the Time Planet—and the subsequent development of the Guardian of Forever and the Time Gate as a research tool—had been to the study of galactic history what the invention of the warp-drive had been to interstellar travel. Kirk could empathize with their special excitement, even if he couldn't wholly share in it.

Of the three, Erickson and Grey were human, Erickson was a small, intense man in his mid-forties, with thinning grey hair cut in bangs in the front—Vulcan style. His limbs seemed to be in constant motion, like the legs of a millipede. The most noticeable facet of his personality was his finding everything, absolutely everything, to be "fine, just fine"—and said so.

Jan Grey was slightly younger, taller and she had a pleasant narrow face that was now glowing with inner anticipation. Both humans wore plain grey jumpsuits emblazoned with the crossed Ionic column and short spade of physical history. They carried elaborate tricorders in shoulder harness.

The third member of the official research party, Loom Aleek-om was neither human nor Vulcan. The native of Aurelia stood head and shoulders above Spock, though he was thinner and lighter than any of them, even Grey.

His wings he kept neatly folded along the line of his back. Short arms ended in a spread of delicately taloned claws, which could manipulate the extremely fine controls on his own, smaller tricorder.

Tattooed on his beak was an intricate scroll—sign of manhood—above which wide, black eyes shone piercingly. They were in startling contrast to his brilliant gold and blue-green plumage.

"Ladies and gentlemen," Kirk smiled, "are you ready?" A rhetorical question. Erickson couldn't resist waving his pudgy arms in reply anyway.

"Ready?" he chirped, feigning disbelief. "We've been ready for days, for months for this minute, Captain! First we encounter that terrible monster and I thought we'd never get here at all. Then more days of unexpected travel and waiting. And you want to know if we're ready?"

"I do not believe I shall ever understand this extraordinary affectation of humans," mused Spock as they took their places in the transporter alcove, "for answering a simple, direct question with half a dozen inane ones."

"Don't worry, Spock," replied Kirk, scratching at his newly grown right palm, "it's not contagious."

"I sincerely hope not, Captain," said Spock fervently.

Beaming down was convenient and quick, though uneventful. They missed the spectacular sights of shuttling down through the silver atmosphere.

No one would miss a descent to the dry, semidesert section they would eventually arrive at, however.

Oddly, very little was know of the early civilizations of the Time Planet itself. Nor of how its inhabitants were able to unite a seething infinitude of time lines and tie them to a single point on their world. Nor why.

Oh, the usual reasons were given . . . curiosity sparked them, and the spirit of scientific exploration. But Kirk and many others couldn't help but believe that the builders of such an incredible device as the Guardian of Forever must have had some other, unknown, more potent reason for constructing it.

There was irony on a grand scale present, too. For in tying together thousands upon thousands of time lines, the builders of the Guardian of Forever had apparently neglected to tie in their *own*. So historians could use the Guardian to research the reasons behind any great invention—except the Guardian.

A distant chance existed that this was not in fact the case, that the time line of the Guardian's inventors was in truth accessible. But if so, it had not yet been discovered. It's builders had covered their own past too well.

The research party materialized at the modest, clean reception station of the Historical Institute. The reception port was fully automated, proceeding on the logic that machines couldn't be bribed. Anyone attempting to beam down to another part of the planet, illegally, would have found himself materialized instead—thanks to elaborate transporter intercepts—inside one of the well-armed armored fortresses that circled the time planet with unceasing, never-tiring vigilance.

The station was near the southern sector of the best preserved portion of the massive urban ruins that rose near the Guardian. The city of Oyya, all two thousand square kilometers of it, was itself a formidable subject for historical and archaeological study.

Excavations had revealed that at one time the city was even greater in extent. And there were ruins of other enormous cities scattered around the planet, many even larger than Oyya. But none were so well preserved.

Had the Time Planet, then, once been severely over-populated? Was the Time Gate a last, desperate means of finding a way to relieve population pressure before it overwhelmed its creators? There was evidence to support such a theory.

Most particularly, despite the unquestionably high degree of civilization attained on this world, there was no hint, no sign that its inhabitants had ever discovered a drive capable of carrying them from star to star. And there were no other planets, uninhabitable or otherwise, in the Time Planet's system. It didn't have even a single moon.

The Time Planet was alone in space. Its visionaries and explorers had been forced to go adventuring in time.

The automatic checkpoints at the reception station were thorough and efficient. As soon as they'd cleared, they were met at the exit lounge by the head of the Institute's main station on the planet, Dr. Vassily.

Dr. Vassily was elderly, silver haired, scintillating of mind, very female, and built like a hockey puck. Notwithstanding, she had the voice of a pixyish eleven-year-old.

She invited them into the nearby central building, a spartan yet comfortable facility, for a light snack and some heavy conversation. Visitors were still a rarity on the Time Planet.

Brandied tea, cake—the tea was good, even if reconstituted. Somehow, though, reconstituted brandied tea, in all its varied brands and types, never approached the real thing. Of course, the natural product was far beyond the financial reach of pioneer historians—however revered and respected.

Kirk forced himself to make easy conversation with the good doctor. It wasn't hard; she was fascinating. But before long Erickson was squirming like a jellyfish with the fidgets, Aleek-om was beginning to flap his wings nervously, sending feathers into everyone's tea, and even the normally imperturbable Jan Grey was showing signs of severe impatience.

"We certainly appreciate your hospitality, Dr. Vassily," Kirk said smoothly and honestly. "But as you can probably tell, my professional charges are anxious to be about their job."

"Of course," she nodded sagely. "Thoughtless of me. I've been working here for so many years I'd forgotten what the experience of a first trip to the Gate means to outsiders." Her voice turned brisk and workmanlike.

"There's a ground car waiting for you outside in the motor-pool hangar. Take the black and yellow one. I've had it pre-checked and fueled for you." She rose, her coveralls falling in shapeless wrinkles around her stout form, and walked them to the door. It stood open to the dry desert air. The climate here sucked moisture from unprepared bodies, but the temperature was not as severe as on other parts of the Time Planet.

She directed her attention to Aleek-om. "By the way, Loom, what time line are you going to search out?" Aleek-om's upper and lower beak clicked several times in rapid succession—a sign of humor among his kind.

"Why, that of the city Oyya's, of course—*cher-wit*!" Dr. Vassily smiled at the in-joke.

"It's been tried, believe me. With every semantic variation you could think of. Every play on words, every stretching of definitions. The Guardian's reply to such requests is always the same.

" 'There is no access through the Gate to the requested time line'." Aleek-om looked suddenly serious.

"Dr. Vassily, do you really think the builders of the Guardian forgot to tie their own time line into the device?"

"No one can say for sure, of course," she replied, wholly professional now. "Personally, I tend to the belief that any race which could construct such an astounding phenomenon as the Guardian would not overlook something that affected them so deeply and so closely. I prefer to think that for their own unknown reasons they denied access to their own past—to themselves and to those who might come after them.

"We may never know the truth, and I want to!" She grinned awkwardly, a little embarrassed at the sudden outburst of emotion.

On the way to the motor-pool hangar, this was commented on. Grey found it unseemly. Aleek-om attributed it

to too little fresh contact with others. Erickson thought it
only human.

Spock, as usual, pinpointed it.

It was called dedication.


The ground car carried them easily and rapidly over
the dry terrain. It was fifteen kilometers from the reception station to the site itself.

There was no Gate, no artificial barrier in evidence
around the Guardian. It had value beyond measure, value
that transcended mere monetary considerations. Anyone
who wished to try and destroy it—if, indeed, it could be
destroyed—might seemingly have free and clear access to
it. It had been demonstrated time and time again that
madmen would attempt most anything.

Nor was there any visible bar to potential misusers of
the device. It seemed that anyone who could manage the
time and expense necessary to reach the Time Planet and
who shuttled instead of beaming down to its surface could
make whatever use of the Gate he wished.

Of course, there was the small matter of slipping past
the four superbly equipped orbital fortresses that covered
every square meter of the planet in a ring of destructive
power. Power reserved elsewhere only for protecting
prime military centers.

It meant avoiding the gigantic phaser and missile batteries buried deep in the innocent-looking sands that
drifted in low dunes around the Guardian itself.

But anyone who could get past that—well, access to the
Time Gate was quite free to all such.

Such elaborate precautions were more than justified.

It would not do to allow the frivolous or unstable access
to the malleable past. So the missiles that remained locked
in their racks and the phasers that sat on their stores of
ravening energy and did not disturb the desert bushes
around them were occasionally publicized. Thus far no
one had yet tempted them.

A well-mounted military expedition might possibly
have succeeded in seizing the Guardian by force, if it
managed to avoid total destruction in the battle that
would ensue with the planetary defenses.

But that would mean war. Access of a belligerent to an enemy's past, well, it was unthinkable. So three empires and two interstellar federations cooperated in policing the Time Planet. They were reassured by the certain knowledge that anyone of them who dared try to make use of the Guardian for its own purposes would invite the immediate wrath of the other four.

It might not have been the most civilized of arrangements, but it worked.

Not that the setting of the Guardian was unimpressive, oh no. Hydrogen missiles might be larger, planet-to-space phasers more intricate, but none could match the nearby city of Oyya for sheer splendor. It stretched on and on, magnificent ruins dominating the horizon as far as one could see to east and south.

And of course, there was the Guardian of Forever itself.

Physically, it was impressive without being massive. Certainly in size it was nothing to match such awe-inspiring artifacts of ancient civilizations as the Temple of Halos on Canabbra IV, or the Aljaddean Wall on Qahtan.

In color it was the shade of rusty iron, spotted here and there with overtones of grey. In shape it resembled a lopsided doughnut. The central hollow of that doughnut was the actual Time Gate. It was always filled with luminous, shifting images of a thousand pasts, all racing by at speeds far too rapid for even scanning tubes to pick out and disseminate.

They left the ground car near a clump of some hearty green-brown desert bushes and walked up until they stood a couple of meters in front of the cut stone base. Kirk and Spock, having been here before, chose instead to spend a moment observing their fellow observers.

Grey just stood there quietly, her eyes shining. Aleekom's wings fluttered gently and thin claws drew small preparatory beeps from his special tricorder. As for Erickson, he shoved both fists into chubby hips, blew out his cheeks, and beamed.

"Well, isn't this *fine*— just *fine*!" he said reverently. He turned to his companions. "Let's get a-move on."

Grey seemed to float back to reality from some distant place. "Yes, by all means. You know the rules." Aleek-om noddded, a thoroughly humanoid gesture.

"Only one of us is permitted to undertake the actual entry and journey with Captain Kirk and Commander Spock acting as supplementary observers and escort. The rest of us will remain here in the present time to record and interpret the subsequent flow of regularized time-sequences."

Then the three historians did a curious thing. They bent over and spent several moments searching the ground. When they stood, each placed his or her open palm face up towards a common center. Two pebbles of varying size lay in each palm.

"All right, get ready" Grey instructed. Hands were placed behind backs, Grey doing likewise.

"I beg your pardon, Captain," murmured Spock curiously, "but what, exactly, is happening?"

"We're going to decide which one of us goes and which two stay behind, Commander," Grey told him.

Spock considered this. "I see—no, I do not see. You will pardon me, Historian Grey. I am not familiar with the intimate interworkings of professionals in your field—so perhaps I should not venture to comment upon them—but this does not strike me as an especially scientific way of determining the composition of this expedition."

Aleek-om shook his feathered head again, set brilliant gold plumes dancing. "If I live for a thousand mating flights, I'll never understand you Vulcans."

"Ready?" queried Grey.

"Ready," the two males echoed.

"Now!"

Each thrust a closed fist into the center of their little circle while Grey counted, "One . . . two . . . three!"

Three hands opened. A single pebble rested in Grey's open palm, another in Aleek-om's.

"Ah, that's fine, colleagues," announced Erickson, "truly fine!" He tossed both his revealed pebbles over his shoulder. They dropped their own, downcast. It didn't last but a moment.

"Well, good luck, old boy," said Aleek-om, and Grey concurred. "Yes, good luck, Theodore."

They proceeded to a solemn shaking of hands. Aleek-om curled his hand in a peculiar way so as not to scratch a sensitive human palm. Then the two unlucky historians began to prepare their tricorders.

"Captain," intoned a thoroughly puzzled Spock, "I confess I am still confused by this method of selection for such an important mission. I don't believe I have witnessed anything quite so arbitrary since . . ."

"I'll explain it all to you later, Mr. Spock," Kirk grinned, "in the future. Right now, Mr. Erickson seems impatient to be on his way."

"Yes, yes," insisted the little historian, waving his warms like a semaphoring turtle, "let's get going."

The other historians turned their tricorder's visual pickups on and aimed them at the flowing Time Gate. Erickson mounted the stone platform and took up a position just in front of it. Kirk flanked him on the right side, Spock on the other. Then his voice boomed out—a squeaky parody of an old-line politician's.

"Guardian of Forever!"

For a long moment nothing happened. Then, from somewhere out of the air in front of them, a ponderous, rolling voice replied. It was heavy with age and weighty with infinite patience. Was this an accumulated effect, from answering thousands of inquiries? Or was it the Guardian's original voice? Kirk wondered. It always responded with perfect fluency to any question, no matter what language it was framed in.

Regardless, the effect produced by those thunderous yet gentle tones was sobering.

The last vestiges of humor disappeared from the little assembly. Everyone was all business now.

"TO WHENCE DO YOU WISH TO TRAVEL, AND FROM WHENCE COME YE," rumbled that mighty voice.

"We come from elsewhere," answered Erickson formally, his words ridiculously inadequate in counterpoint to that stentorian thunder. "And we wish the elsewhen of the Empire of Orion."

The Empire of Orion! Kirk started. He'd never bothered to inquire which time line the historians intended to explore. They hadn't struck him as a particularly adventurous bunch. Erickson's request came as a double surprise.

He'd figured this group of academicians for something much duller and more mundane than this. Say, the Butterfly Wars of Lepidopt, or the ceramic- and porcelain-making era of Sang Ho Hihn.

But, the Empire of Orion!

He found himself getting just a little bit excited. This was going to be rather more fun than he'd anticipated.

There was a clouding effect obscuring the Gate. A creamy blue-green blur filmed over the hazy surface of the circular center. As it did so, the dizzying array of time scenes began to slow. It was like watching a projector gradually wind down from a high speed—the visual equivalent of a slowing tape.

Eventually only a single alien scene remained. It did not shift, did not ripple, but held steady and clear. The blur started to fade. As it did so it was replaced in the scene by natural colors.

When they passed through the Time Gate, their first task would be to obtain a change of clothing. In the barbaric Empire of Orion, two starship uniforms and the casual dress of Historian Erickson would render them something less than inconspicuous. No one knew what passed for casual dress in that time period. Kirk knew this was so because if they *did* know, the historians would have had their necessary costumes prepared in advance.

Fortunately, the medium of exchange was only gold, and Erickson was amply supplied. They'd have no trouble making any needed purchases. Erickson was probably pleased. It gave him an excuse to bring back three sets of the genuine article—for study, of course. It was forbidden to profit materially from a journey through the Gate. Otherwise, the most dedicated researcher might be tempted to travel back in time to, say Earth's past and return with some little valuable knickknack like Praxiteles lost gold statue of Pallas Athena.

They could touch things, move about, and purchase,

but nothing of real value could be brought back except for study purposes.

Once through, they would spend some thirty minutes objective time. That might be several days in the subjective time of the Orionic Empire. Then, wherever they happened to be in space in that ancient civilization, the Guardian would reach out and pull them back to the present, ejecting them once more on silent desert sands.

Thirty minutes! Even the great, still unexplained energies that powered the Guardian could not hold open a time vortex any longer than that. And the amount of power necessary to hold a time dilation for even five minutes objective time was nothing short of astronomical. It was generally agreed on that the Guardian somehow drew directly on the local sun for power—but exactly how this was accomplished was still a source of mystery and controversy.

"Captain Kirk, Commander Spock," piped Erickson, "if you're ready, gentlemen?"

"Whenever you are, Mr. Erickson," acknowledged Kirk. Erickson turned to glance back behind himself.

"Ready, colleagues?"

"Ready, short stuff," grinned Grey.

"Go get 'em, Ted," cheered Aleek-om.

"Then, gentlemen," he said importantly to Kirk and Spock, "if you will, on three—one, two, three . . ." They stepped forward.

Two seekers of knowledge . . . one human, the other faintly so, stood alone on the sandy plain where a moment before they had been five. Two seekers of knowledge— and one interested onlooker. McCoy had chosen to remain quietly in the background.

The early Empire civilization turned out to be a maelstrom of colors and sights and fascinating detail through which Kirk, Spock, and the little historian moved like wraiths in a dream. The sounds matched the barbaric imagery—the unexpected and incredible exceeded the wildest expectations. They spent two and a half days, Orion time.

When their thirty real minutes were up, seemingly seconds later, Kirk was as sorry to leave as Erickson.

One moment they were changing clothes in the back-room of a disreputable inn in a gaudy bazaar, while meters away an equally disreputable personage was auctioning off modest examples of local feminine pulchritude. The next, they were standing once again on the stone platform facing the Guardian.

Grey and Aleek-om made no move to approach them as the three travelers swayed uneasily. There was always a moment or two of nausea that followed any passage through a time vortex. Then their systems had readjusted to the sudden change in climate and gravity and other variables, and they stood easily once again.

Both historians appeared excited and pleased by the stream of slowed time pictures from different time-sequences that they'd been able to examine and record. Apparently that had been exciting enough. No one seemed the least upset now at being left behind.

Erickson, for his part, was flushed with a glow that on a more imposing individual might have been interpreted as maniacal.

Kirk noticed McCoy staring at Spock. There was an expression of mild concern and some puzzlement on the doctor's face. Studious physician to the end, the Captain reflected.

Come to think of it, Aleek-om and Grey also seemed to be staring at the science officer. But in the first flush of excitement at their successful journey and return, Kirk didn't notice the intensity of their stares. For that matter, neither did Spock or Erickson.

"Relax, Bones, we're all fine. Usual upset stomach, and that's all but gone. Orion at the dawn of civilization, Bones! Just watching, not interacting significantly for fear of changing some tiny bit of history . . ." He paused. The others were paying absolutely no attention to him. Instead, they continued to stare at Spock.

For the first time, Kirk took notice of their odd fascination with his assistant.

"What's the matter?" He still smiled. "Bones, what's wrong?"

Dr. McCoy did a rather startling thing, then. He jerked his head in Spock's direction, then pointed at him. His voice was open, curious.

"Who's he, Jim?"

This outrageous comment took some time to register. Kirk looked over at Spock reflexively. It was the same old Spock, all right, down to his unwavering expression and peaked aural receptors.

For his part, Spock's eyebrows made an upward leap of Olympian proportions. In fact, the science officer looked as close to total befuddlement as Kirk could ever recall having seen him. The captain turned back to McCoy, mildly irritated. The excitement of their return had been stolen from him.

"What do you mean, 'Who's he?' You know Mr. Spock."

McCoy's nonchalant attitude and indifferent manner were much more shocking than his casual reply.

" 'Fraid I don't, Jim."

Spock's expression changed only slightly at that. Just the veriest hint, the merest touch of annoyance seeped through his otherwise stony visage.

Kirk, however, was much more expressive in his display of facial contortions. He started to speak further to McCoy, became aware of his imminent loss of self-control, and thought better of speaking just now. There was no point in getting upset, yet.

It was a practical joke. Yes, of course! Bones probably authored the whole thing himself. It would fall apart any minute, as soon as someone made a slip and said something relating to Spock. For now he would go along with the gag. He pulled out his communicator, flipped open the grid, and glanced over at Grey and Aleek-om.

"You've both concluded your observations, then?" Jan Grey sighed reluctantly. That was the most blatant show of emotion she had yet displayed. Maybe she had Vulcan blood.

"Sadly, yes, Captain. It was all too short, too brief. But yes, our work here is finished."

They all climbed back into the shuttle car. Kirk, Spock, and McCoy rode in silence while the three historians chattered in the back.

"We should stop before we depart and thank Dr. Vassily for her help and consideration," noted Aleek-om when they'd returned the car to its stall in the main hangar.

Erickson agreed. "Yes, by all means." He nodded vigorously. Kirk interposed a negative as he toyed with his open communicator. He'd put off calling the ship. Erickson's call to remain here longer woke him from idle daydreams.

"Why not, Captain?" The stout researcher was pouting. Then he smiled slyly. "That brandied tea wasn't half bad, even if it was reconstituted."

"It's not the quality of the refreshments, Erickson. There's something else." Kirk looked around at the now curious faces.

At first they'd all stared with unconcealed fascination at Spock. Now they were studiously ignoring him. If this was a practical joke, then someone was carrying it off in style. Too much style. Kirk was starting to feel that any overtones of humor to the situation were becoming shaded in tones of black.

He activated the communicator. Anyone could beam freely up from the surface of the Time Planet. Getting *down* was the problem.

"Kirk to *Enterprise*."

"*Enterprise*," came a familiar voice with sharp vowel sounds. So Scotty was working with Chief Kyle on the transporter now. So much the better.

"Six to beam up, Scotty."

"Aye, sir."

Aleek-om had been thinking. Now he spoke delicately to Kirk.

"If you don't mind, Captain, I should like to remain here a while longer, to record and study some of the artifacts Dr. Vassily has unearthed. If we have some time before departure, that is." The Aurelian's expression was hopeful.

"Me too, Captain," added Jan Grey. Kirk nodded, turned to the other historian.

"How about you, Erickson?"

"Oh no, I'm satisfied. All I want to do is put my tapes in a big viewer and play them back. I was so busy recording and taking notes that I didn't have half a chance to enjoy the journey." His blissful look turned momentarily serious.

"But you've got to understand, Captain Kirk, that this is a once-in-a-lifetime experience for most historians. We can't hold you up." Aleek-om and Grey indicated agreement. "I know starship time is precious. But if my compatriots could have even a few additional minutes . . ."

"All right, all right." Kirk grinned, spoke into the communicator. "Cancel that, Scotty. Four only to come up. Myself, Mr—" he hesitated, "and the others."

The two historians who would remain a while longer thanked him profusely and then hurried off toward the reception station. They promised to be ready for transporter pickup at the first call from the orbiting *Enterprise*.

"All clear, Scotty. Bring us up."

"Aye, sir."

There was a familiar feeling of disorientation. The four figures dissolved into four roughly cylindrical columns of luminescent particles.

In the transporter room, Chief Engineer Scott personally handled the delicate task of transporting while Chief Transporter Kyle, himself a master at the job, watched admiringly. Those calloused, practiced hands operated the transporter controls even more smoothly than his own.

The first thing Kirk noticed when he regained sight was the startled expression on his chief engineer's face. The first thing he heard when he regained hearing was the startled tone of his chief engineer's voice.

"Captain—" Scott paused, unmistakably confused. "I was expecting two of the historians with you and Dr. McCoy. But a Vulcan—"

Kirk decided that was quite enough. If this was a practical joke, it was going too far.

"Explain yourself, Mr. Scott!" he snapped. Scott's mouth worked. His puzzlement seemed honest.

"S . . . sir?"

Kirk chewed at his lower lip and stepped out of the alcove, off the platform.

"I don't know what's going on here—but the first officer of this ship will be treated with respect!"

"Captain," came a strange voice from the elevator, "I assure you no one has ever treated me otherwise."

It was Kirk's turn to look dumbfounded.

His gaze snapped to the right. The humanoid who'd just brazenly laid claim to Spock's title walked easily into the room. He was an Andorian, clad in the blue shirt of starfleet science officer, and wearing the insignia of a full commander.

Like most Andorians he was slim, rather fragile-looking, and had the pale blue eyes and silver hair of most of his people. Kirk noticed the two slightly curved, flaring antennae which protruded from his forehead and ended in dull, round knobs. These were his organs of hearing. He had no shell-shaped ears as did human or Vulcan.

Where distance was involved the knobbed antennae had less range than other humanoid sensing organs, but they could pick up much higher and lower frequencies. The Andorian's slim build belied his agility and strength, characteristics which certain other races had learned about the hard way.

Kirk took a couple of steps towards this alien, and his jaw dropped in amazement. He looked the other up and down without fazing him, finally managed to blurt out his thoughts.

"Who the hell are you?" This time it was Dr. McCoy who replied, wryly.

"I thought sure you'd know Thelin by now, Jim. He's been your first officer for five years."

"Is something the matter, Captain?" queried the Andorian. His tones were soft, slightly accented. And he too seemed openly puzzled. Kirk could only stare at him.

Spock finally broke the silence, summing up both his own and Kirk's thoughts in his usual terse fashion.

"Captain, I have come to the conclusion that this is not a game."

"No—no," Kirk muttered. "I agree, Mr. Spock. But if it's a reality—and everyone else here seems to think it is—then what happened?" He stiffened.

"All right, I don't know what's going on here, but I'm going to get to the bottom of it! Spock, Mr. . . . Thelin. If you'll both come with me to the main briefing room.

There's no point in upsetting anyone else on board." They started off.

"Me too, Captain?" asked Erickson. He had no real part in the problem, but if something was the matter with Spock—well, he'd formed enough of a friendship with the starship officers to at least be concerned.

"Yes, by all means, Mr. Erickson, join us."

# VII

The command briefing room was small, with a single free-formed table of dark mahoganylike wood from the forests of IandB dominating the center. Holographic portraits of various alien landscapes decorated the walls, along with a framed copy of the Federation charter, and there was a musical rain sculpture shifting and chiming softly in one corner.

The seats were also free-formed, lush and comfortable, but they could do little to ease the tenseness of the four humanoids who now sat in them.

Erickson immediately set to work with his tricorder, keeping his verbal requests to the machine to a whisper. He had thought about the unbelievable situation, and decided that maybe the compact instrument had noticed something significant they had not remembered.

"I will pass over the obvious, gentlemen," began Kirk. "I can think of only one explanation for what seems to have happened, and I'm sure it has occurred to you also."

"When we were in the time vortex, something happened to change the present as we know it. No one seems to recognize Mr. Spock. And neither he nor I nor Mr. Erickson recognizes Mr. Thelin. The only answer must be that the past was somehow altered when we were in it. Instead of emerging into our own time line, Mr. Spock, Mr. Erickson, and myself have reemerged into an alternate secondary one as a result of that as yet unidentified change." He paused for breath.

"And if that sounds confusing, gentlemen, I assure you it's a fit description of my present state of mind."

Erickson chose that moment to interrupt. He shook his head and looked disappointed.

"Nothing, Captain Kirk. I've just done a double-speed review of our entire journey. The tricorder has no record of anything we did while in the vortex that could conceivably have affected the future. *Any* future."

"Please, Mr. Erickson," requested Kirk. "I don't doubt your readings. But could you . . . try once more? Take all the time you need."

"I don't need any more time, Captain. I've done this sort of review a thousand times before." He shrugged, bent over the tricorder once more.

When he looked up again a while later, after completing the second run-through, the stocky historian found all eyes were on him. The sameness of his expression was eloquent.

"Nothing, Captain. I've even run down any changes in the atmospheric content while we were present, and there's absolutely nothing."

Kirk slammed a fist down on the smooth wood. One of these days he was going to break a hand doing that.

"But, dammit—*something* was changed!"

"It seems, Captain," interposed Spock easily, "that I am the only one affected. The mission, the ship, the crew—except for myself—remain the same."

"Not entirely, Mr. Spock," Kirk countered. "I still know who you are. So does Erickson." The historian nodded vigorously. "But no one else aboard does. While we were in Orion's past, the time revision that apparently occurred here didn't affect us." He looked thoughtful. "I wonder how extensive it is?"

"If you'll pardon me, Jim," began Thelin. Then he smiled faintly, uncomfortably. "Captain, I might be able to answer that. While we were on our way down here, I took the liberty of placing an informational request with the library. It should tell us how complete the time change has been."

"I didn't hear you put in any request, Mr. Thelin."

"You were in deep conversation with Mr. . . . Spock, at the time," the Andorian replied.

As if on cue, the bosun's whistle sounded in the room. Thelin looked pleased.

"That ought to be the reply now." Kirk pressed a half-hidden switch under the rim of the table. A three-sided viewer popped up from the center of the dark wood. He hit another switch.

"Kirk here."

The picture of a young, neatly turned-out ensign appeared on the three screens. The ensign started to speak, but Kirk waved him off.

"Just a minute, Ensign." He turned to Spock. "You know who that is, Mr. Spock?"

"Ensign Bates, Captain. Inexperienced, but studious, well-intentioned, reasonably efficient. Graduated OTS Starfleet with high honors but not the highest. Served one year apprenticeship on the shuttle tender SCOPUS. Transferred to *Enterprise* starda . . ."

"That'll do, Spock." Kirk looked satisfied.

"That would approximate my own evaluation of Bates' abilities at this stage, Captain," Thelin added casually. "Transferred to *Enterprise* stardate 5365.6."

"Ummm." Kirk's tone was noncommittal. He directed his attention back to the screen. "What have you got for us, Ensign?"

"Sir, we've checked Starfleet records as Commander Thelin requested."

Even though he thought he was growing used to the present impossible situation, Kirk still gave a little mental jump every time he heard the Andorian referred to by his own crew as "Commander Thelin." Deep down he knew that—in the original time line, at least—the Andorian didn't really exist.

Or was *this* the real time line, and the other merely a secondary copy? One problem at a time . . .

Yet McCoy, Scotty—everyone—seemed to know Thelin intimately, and not Mr. Spock.

He blinked, remembered Bates. The ensign was patiently awaiting Kirk's orders to report the researched material, destroy it, stand on his head, play dead, or do *something*.

"Findings, Ensign?" he said crisply. The ensign's reply had the directness of truth.

"There is no Vulcan named Spock listed with Starfleet in any capacity, sir. Neither as commander, nor cook—no listing whatsoever."

Spock's only visible reaction was the moderate ascension of one eyebrow.

"I see," Kirk muttered. He thought a moment, then, "You have your visual pickup on?"

"Of course, Captain. I was not told this was to be a closed meetin . . ."

"No, no, it's not. Relax, Ensign. Now, can you see the Vulcan sitting to my immediate right?" Bates' head and eyes moved. He showed no reaction.

"Yes, sir."

"Do you recognize him?"

"No, sir," responded Bates, who was one of Spock's regular science-library assistants. "I've never seen him before in my life."

Thelin leaned forward and addressed the screen. "Did you also research the Vulcan family history requested?"

"Yes, Commander," said the ensign crisply. "There are some related visual materials. I can put them on the viewer pickup, if you wish."

"We so wish, Ensign," Kirk ordered. Bates hit a button below screen pickup level and his image vanished, to be replaced immediately by a still hologram of a distinguished-looking male Vulcan clad in formal ambassadorial attire. Bates continued to speak.

"This is Sarek of Vulcan, ambassador to seventeen Federation planets in the past thirty t-standard years."

Spock broke into the Ensign's speech. "That is not correct."

Kirk only grinned sardonically.

"In this case—or this time, Mr. Spock—it seems that it

is." Spock gave a slight nod of understanding and looked back to the tripartite viewer.

"I wish to ask a question."

"Yes, Commander?" Bates might not know Spock, but he could still recognize the uniform and rank of a starship commander, even if not his own.

"What of Sarek's family? His wife and son?"

The picture of Sarek disappeared, to be replaced by another hologram. This one was of a lovely human woman in her early thirties. She was fair-haired and slim, delicate—one of those rare women who you know instantly will retain her youthfulness well into old age. The young officer's voice—impersonal voice, doom voice, continued—

"Amanda, wife of Sarek, known on Earth as Amanda Grayson." Kirk gave Spock a sympathetic look as Bates droned on. "The couple separated after the death of their son."

That finally drew a visible reaction from Spock, though, as Kirk knew, ninety percent of it was still bound up tightly inside his first officer. Bates continued.

"The wife was killed in a shuttle accident at Lunaport, on her way home to Earth. Ambassador Sarek has not remarried."

Everyone was watching Spock now, and he was watching none of them. His eyes remained glued to the picture on the screen. When he finally did speak, there was a pause, a bare hint of a catch in his voice that could have been—no, ridiculous.

"My mother—" he whispered softly. Then he spoke—well, almost normally. There was no uncertainty in his tone, only a desire to satisfy perverse curiosity to the utmost, to draw out the thing to its ultimate mad conclusion.

"The son—what was his name and age when he died?"

"Spock," came Bates reply. "Age . . ." he seemed to be checking some off-screen reference, ". . . age seven."

"Sympathy is not among my race's primary traits, Mr. Spock," said Thelin, "but I believe I can understand a little of what you are feeling now. I'm sorry, truly I am." He gave the Andorian equivalent of a shrug. "But I am me and you are you, and there is nothing to be done for it."

"Not in this time line, no," mused Kirk.

"You are, of course, correct, Captain," Spock added. "But if we didn't change anything in the past—"

"We didn't!" insisted Erickson. "We didn't!" Suddenly his forehead creased and he repeated, softly this time,

"We didn't!" insisted Erickson. "We didn't!" Suddenly

"Of course! Jan and Loom!"

"Surely," said Spock, "they didn't enter the Guardian while we were in the vortex?"

"No, no!" Erickson was nervous as a mouse. "They would never do a thing as potentially dangerous as that. But scanning—they must have been scanning! We might at least get some useful information from them if they . . ."

". . . were looking into my past while we were in Orion's. Yes, I see what you are leading toward, Historian." Spock rose, looked at Kirk.

"Captain, we must go down to the Guardian again. And as quickly as possible. The longer we stay in this time line, the stronger our position here grows, and the less chance we have of returning to and correcting our own—my own."

"Certainly, Spock. Erickson, come on!" The four rose and left the briefing room.

"You're sure you don't recognize him?" Kirk asked Scott when they'd returned to the transporter room. They were mounting the transporter platform prior to beam-down. Scott studied Spock carefully, indifferently, and shook his head.

"There are few Vulcans on the *Enterprise*, Captain. I'm not likely to forget any, let alone a commander."

"Thanks, Scotty. Beam us down, please."

On the way back to the Guardian in the ground car, they tried to explain the situation to Grey and Aleek-om. Since Kirk was still confused himself, he wasn't sure they made things much clearer to the two historians who had remained behind. But they seemed to grasp the idea behind what had happened better than he had. Time was their business, space was his.

Of course, neither of them recognized Mr. Spock. And both seemed to know Thelin. The Andorian had insisted on coming along, as was his privilege both as commander and science officer.

By the time they had returned to the quiescent Guardian of Forever, mutual agreement had reached on an approximation of sequential probabilities. Nevertheless, Kirk continued to examine every salient fact with the three historians as they all made their way toward the Guardian. As always, the Time Gate was modest in appearance, overwhelming in capabilities.

Glowing cream-colored mists flowed and danced patiently, langorously in the central hollow, oblivious to the petty problems of the small knot of approaching humanoids.

"If we didn't change anything while we were in the time vortex," Kirk insisted, "someone or something else must have." He turned to Aleek-om and then Grey. "You were using the Guardian while we were gone."

"Yes, but it was nothing unusual," said Grey matter-of-factly. "We were merely scanning occasional sequences of recent history."

"Any recent Vulcan history?" asked Kirk.

"Why, yes!" She smiled in sudden realization. "I see the way your thoughts have been going, Captain. I don't see what we might have done, but—of course it seems the only other possibility."

"What time period?" asked Spock as they mounted the last step leading towards the Gate.

"I'm not sure." She fumbled with the omnipresent tricorder. "Just a momnet . . ." A quick recheck provided the desired information. "No specific dates listed—approximately twenty to thirty Vulcan years past." Kirk had a sudden thought. His question beat Spock's by a few seconds.

"Was there any notation recorded on the death of the son of a Vulcan ambassador named Sarek and his human wife?" Both historians looked thoughtful, glanced at each other before turning back to Kirk and Spock.

"I don't recall any, but there was so much information—" Aleek-om looked a little tense as he worked his own tricorder. Thin, powerful claws clicked over the sensitive controls, too fine for any human to manipulate. It hummed softly, then stopped.

Aleek-om jabbed a recessed switch, ran something back and played through it more slowly. The hum deepened. He stopped again and nodded, his crest bobbing and dancing in the dry desert breeze.

"*Cher-wit!* Yes, the death is indeed recorded."

"How . . ." Kirk all but choked on the peculiar-sounding words, "how did he die?" He still found it hard to believe he was living this nightmare. It was no consolation to know that it must be a hundred times worse for Spock.

Again, Aleek-om checked the instrument readings.

"The child is recorded as dying during some form of . . . maturity test. Yes, that's it. It is recorded only because the father was a notable figure in government and in Federation history."

Spock spoke absently. "The Kahs-wan—a survival test for young males. It is traditional, a holdover from less peaceful, less civilized days."

"The death is recorded as—" Aleek-om continued, but Spock finished it for him.

". . . falling on the twentieth day of Tasmeen." All but Kirk and Erickson looked at Spock in surprise.

"How do you know this?" asked Thelin. Spock paused, spoke slowly.

"That was the day my—my cousin saved my life when I was attacked in the desert by a wild animal."

But how could Spock know that that was the particular day and that that incident was crucial?

Inspiration hit Kirk then, wthout warning—at warp-eight speed.

"This cousin, Spock, what was his name?" Spock frowned, shifted his position on the rocky surface underfoot.

"That I do not seem to recall clearly. I was very young. He called himself—yes, Selek. A common enough name in my father's family. He was visiting us." Spock frowned slightly. "Odd, but I never saw him again after that—though I wished to, many times. Nor, I believe, did any of my family." The frown grew deeper.

"Captain, your expression, I believe you . . ." Spock seemed to hesitate.

Kirk looked directly at his first officer. Inside, Spock *knew.* But he was so close to the answer that it hadn't yet come to him.

"Spock—this Selek—did he by any chance look like you do . . . now?"

Even then, Spock was reluctant to accept the idea. Alternative lines of possibility, however, suddenly looked more barren than ever. He nodded slowly.

"I believe he did, Captain. And I see what you are thinking. That other time, it wasn't my 'cousin' who saved me—it was I. I saved myself."

"But this time," continued Kirk, pushing the thought forward, "you were in Orion's past with Mr. Erickson and me. At the same time, Aleek-om and Grey were here, playing back that section of Vulcan history. You couldn't exist in two time lines simultaneously, so you had to vanish from one of them. In other words, you had to die as a boy, since you couldn't be there to save yourself." He shook his head. Much more thinking along paradoxical lines like that and they'd all be candidates for the silly station. He spun to face the Gate.

"Guardian, did you hear that?"

The shifting colors seemed to flow a little faster, shine a touch brighter. When it spoke, the colors pulsed with internal light as each syllable was intoned. The words themselves were, as always, neither masculine nor feminine nor even machinelike—but instead a kind of strange sexless and timeless neuter.

"I HEAR ALL."

"We could resort to the *Enterprise*'s computers," Kirk murmured, as much to himself as to the Gate, "but in all the Universe, no one, nothing, knows as much about time as you. Tell me—is it possible for Spock the Vulcan to return to the period when he was not (God, this was insane!) and repair the broken time line so that all is the same as it was before our last journey?"

A pause, then, "IT IS POSSIBLE," the Guardian boomed indifferently, "IF NO OTHER MAJOR FACTOR HAS BEEN CHANGED. OR IS CHANGED IN THE CHANGING."

Kirk turned to his science officer.

"Do you remember enough, Spock? You heard the Guardian. You can't risk changing anything when you go back. You've got to repeat what happened when you were seven years old."

Spock shook his head slowly, the strain of recall showing plainly.

"I do not remember everything, Captain. There are vague memories, from a child's point of view. But as is common to youthful memories, a child's details are blurred and run together. The memory *is* there—but slightly out of focus."

"You'll have to try!" Kirk insisted. "For you—and your mother—to live." Spock nodded slowly, considering.

"Yes. I will need the following items: a Vulcan desert soft-suit and boots, and a small selection of plain street-wear accessories circa—8877 Vulcan years. The matching obligatory carry-bag should be of the same period and look well used."

"You've got them," nodded Kirk quickly. "I'll have quartermaster section drop whatever they're doing and run them off now." He flipped open his communicator and moved slightly to one side. The three historians were already engaged in animated discussion of what had become for them a fascinating socio-mathematical exercise in conflicting time lines.

This curiosity was touched with tragedy only for Erickson, since among the arguing historians only he had been intimately involved with the actual expedition into Orion's past. But his academic concern outweighed the desire to offer further consolation to Spock. He wasn't very good at such things, anyway.

That left Spock alone with his quiet doppelganger—Thelin. The Andorian studied him closely.

"This proposed modification of time lines will put you in my place on a different plane . . . replace another Thelin somewhere." He paused. "Yet, I am not aggrieved."

"Andorians are noted for many things," said Spock conversationally. "However, as you yourself admitted, sympathy is not one of them."

"True," Thelin nodded. "A warrior race has few sympathies and little time for same. Yet it is not a normal situation we find ourselves in. I, personally, do not feel threatened. Yet, in a way, I am actually contributing to the murder of a distant cousin."

"Who should not be there in the first place," concluded Spock evenly.

"Perhaps. Yet one empathy we Andorians do possess is for family. On this time plane, you will lose—and so would your mother. The knowledge that this will be prevented, at least, is acceptable mental compensation for me."

He gave Spock a smart Vulcan hand salute. "Live long and prosper in your own world, Commander Spock—in your own time." Spock returned the salute.

"And you in yours, Commander Thelin."

There was nothing to do now but wait for Spock's requested clothing and materials to be sent down from the *Enterprise*. There'd be no problem there—planetary defenses could recognize the difference between a suit of clothes and a photon torpedo. But it left them with nothing to do but think, and after a while that wasn't too comfortable for the historians, either.

The little group spent several nervous, awkward minutes wandering around the base of the now familiar Guardian. Kirk studied it idly.

Certainly it possessed some strange unknown variety of organic/inorganic intelligence—witness its answers to questions in many languages. But no one knew if this intelligence lay dormant until evoked. Might it not be always alert, constantly observing? Was it even now looking down on them from some uncomprehensible alien Olympus and musing on their problems? He could ask, of course.

But the Guardian of Forever did not deign to answer any questions about anything but time.

As for other sights to study, they were too far from Oyya for the city's ancient and distant attractions to hold their interest for very long. The area around the Guardian itself was singularly barren.

Even the Time Gate was beginning to seem like no more than a pile of oddly hewn rocks and stone by the time a small transporter effect, a chromatic glow of atomic action, began to take shape nearby. As it faded, the glow congealed into the form of a Vulcan carry-all bag, a small pile of goods and knickknacks, boots, and a neatly tied bundle of sand-colored clothes.

"Nice to know that the crew in this time plane is efficient, too," Kirk commented appreciatively. He hesitated, then held out a hand to Spock. Words were unnecessary.

It took Spock a few moments to make the change of clothing. He stacked his uniform and boots neatly to one side, then turned and moved away from them, walking up to the base of the Gate itself.

Thelin moved to stand next to Kirk. Not wont to miss even a blurred glimpse of what might take place, the three historians activated their own special tricorders. Spock's voice as he addressed the enigmatic intelligence known as the Guardian was clear and precise, as always.

"I wish to visit the planet Vulcan."

"TIME?" rumbled the Guardian.

"Thirty Vulcan years past, the month of Tasmeen, before—before the twentieth day."

There, that ought to provide a reasonable margin of time in which to get reacquainted with himself.

"LOCATION?"

"Just outside the border city of ShiKahr."

By way of reply, the pastel mists that filled the circular Gate started to swirl and boil, flowing slower and slower, until the blur of time pictures began to steady as the Guardian locked in to the requested time line. Then, abruptly, the Gate was filled with a view so familiar to Spock that it immediately relaxed all inner tensions.

A hot, dry, orange world—Vulcan.

"Yes," was all Kirk heard him say—though there seemed to be other words, voiced too low to be understood.

"TIME AND PLACE," the Guardian shouted in tones as stable and final as the Universe, "ARE READY TO RECEIVE YOU."

"Yes," Spock murmured again. One word worth a thousand pictures. Then he was running, running forward, and taking a short leap into the time portal.

His body faded from view as though he were slipping into a transparent sponge. As soon as he touched the field, the picture began to blur from the temporary distortion of the time vortex.

For several moments after he'd vanished, Kirk stood staring at the now resumed blur of time-patterns racing across the Gate. Then he turned to one side, where the blue uniform of a Starfleet commander, science section, and a pair of boots—Starfleet standard issue, officer's—lay on the broken gravel, awaiting their owner's return.

In another, unknown time line, another James T. Kirk was staring at another set of clothes, thinking the same thoughts, hoping the same hopes. And on a different line, perhaps, yet a different Kirk. And another, and another—an infinitude of Kirks waiting for the return of a billion Spocks in a million variations of a certain awkward second or two in time . . . .

Spock stood on the sands of the world of his birth. Behind him, the land was desert, painted in harsh ocher-yellows and umber-browns—spotted only reluctantly here and there by an occasional winsome patch of greenery.

Further back, a range of forbidding black mountains clawed at the sky with great ragged talons of granite, basalt, and gneiss. The thin atmosphere inspired a roof of flinty orange-red instead of the soft blues of Earth. But the clouds that spotted it were just as cottony white.

Before him lay the city of ShiKahr, like a neat, orderly oasis in the wastes. A wide band of lush, landscaped parkland formed a civilizing barrier between urban environment and raw, arid sands. Flowers and other vegetation tended toward soft, warm hues of yellow and brown, with a few isolated sprinklings of pink or purple.

The park buffer zone was as modern as the rest of ShiKahr, which nevertheless was an old city. Buildings were geometric, regular, and aesthetically as well as architecturally sound. A logical city designed for relentlessly logical inhabitants.

A person standing next to Spock at that moment might have heard him mutter something vaguely like, "thirty years . . ." Or it might have been the wind rippling through a desert bush.

In any case, no one could have stood close enough to

see what was going through Spock's mind. That mind was considering. From here on, he was quite aware that his very continued existence depended on repeating with as much precision as possible events he could barely remember, events that had taken place thirty years ago—now.

He shifted the carry-bag higher on his shoulder, ran his right thumb underneath the strap, and started off towards the city. At the city gate he experienced an instant of apprehension. There was always an outside chance that something else about him, something unseen but vital, had been altered by the interlocution of time lines.

If the automatic sentry defense systems which were designed to keep out fierce desert carnivores sensed anything suspicious about him, he would be, not killed, but immobilized and held helplessly tranquilized until the arrival of a detention squad from the city reasoning force.

That wouldn't be fatal. But subsequent questions and examinations could be embarrassing as well as time delaying. At the very least, serious alterations in this time line might be produced. That could jumble matters beyond repair.

They might be damaged beyond change already, but there was little benefit to that line of thought. Besides, it was very depressing.

He needn't have worried. Unseen radiation probed him, hidden sensors clucked approving mechanical tongues. His shape and composition were familiar—Vulcan. No challenge was offered as he walked through the park. No tranquilizing darts *phocked* out at him, no stun rays sought to bar his passage.

He experienced no difficulties whatsoever. His only barrier to progress was confusion of a mental variety. He'd forgotten the beauty of ShiKahr. The calm efficiency and palpable sense of security that made a Vulcan city so different from the hectic, albeit exciting urban hodgepodges of so many other humanoid worlds.

He passed by the last of the flowers, past a gentle fountain that dispensed a constant stream of fresh well water, and suddenly found himself on a walking street.

This pathway was broad and paved, but designed for pedestrian use only. It was quiet and tree-shaded. Every

effort—every stone, every bush, all but the actual place-
ment of the leaves on the branches—was predesigned and
executed to enhance one's serene appreciation of podal
locomotion.

High walls kept homes and gardens discreetly secluded
from passersby. Delicate symmetrical blossoms on creeping vines trailed over many of the stone walls and brightened the rustic scene even further. There was a main ar-
tery in the distance ahead, busy with ground-car activity.
Old-style, outmoded ground-cars, he noted.

That mechanical sound was distant. But soon, another
clamor reached his ears. A group of young voices—male.
Their tone was biting and sarcastic—a near-emotion to
which even Vulcan youth were not immune. The words
matched the tone of delivery.

"Barbarian . . . Earther . . . throwback . . . emotional,
squalling, uncontrolled *Earther!*"

He'd heard those same insults long ago, it seemed. Surprising how painful they could still be, after all those
years. He moved to a corner, turned it, and looked ahead.

A high wall fronted on an intersection of several small
pathways. He moved a few steps further, halting in front
of a high, solid old gate of polished, engraved wood.
Nearby, another lower gateway led to a flourishing garden. In front of this second gate stood a very young version of himself.

There was no question of who it was. Inwardly, he'd
dreaded this moment—from an intellectual, not an emotional, standpoint. How would he react to the first sight of
. . . himself? Kirk had equated it to an old terran expression—being "on the outside looking in." Now that Spock
was actually confronted with the experience, the result
proved anticlimactic.

There was no abrupt sundering of mind, no shattering
of preconceived images. No, no emotional damage. This
younger, smaller version of himself was only a young boy
who looked somehow familiar. But another person entirely.

After all, he'd met a universe full of aliens—and to an
adult, children are often the most alien of all.

He blinked. Three other Vulcan youngsters stood in

front of young Spock, taunting him. Old memories came drifting back, long-lost little pains that made small wrenching tugs deep in his mind.

That one, there, with the light-colored hair—that must be Stark. Then Sofek, next to him, and the tallest one standing between them had to be Sepek—a persistent childhood tormentor until later years, when they grew to become great friends.

But for now . . .

"You're a terran, Spock," shouted Stark. "You could never be a true Vulcan."

"That's not true!" yelled young Spock in reply, barely managing to keep a grip on his temper. "My father . . ."

Sepek's reply touched each noun, each syllable, with contempt.

"Terran! Your father brought shame to Vulcan! Marrying an Earther wom——"

That was more than enough for young Spock. Sadly, his physical reaction was more emotional than reasoned. He rushed forward blindly, arms flailing, to crush and rend his tormentors. Old Spock's first reaction was to observe that one against three—with one of the three much older, heavier, and more experienced—was an illogical arrangement to aggravate. Not to mention an unnecessary one.

But he'd been different as a youngster. Now the rather astonishing emotional outbursts of childhood rushed back to him. Had he really been so ready to react belligerently to mere words? Had he actually been so impulsive, so blind, so—so emotional? There was no denying the evidence of his eyes.

Any last concerns he might have felt about meeting his younger self disappeared. The child really was a different person.

Any mother could have told him that.

Sepek the nearest and strongest, easily dodged young Spock's blind, angry punch. Sepek deftly tripped him backwards while avoiding the clumsy grab. Young Spock landed unceremoniously on his backside in the smooth dirt.

He didn't appear to be hurt—not physically, anyway. Sepek's voice dripped contempt.

"You haven't even mastered a simple Vulcan neck pinch yet!" he said nastily, concluding with the ultimate insult, "Earther!" The three youths walked quietly away.

Young Spock sat there in the settling dust, alone and insulted and hurt, obviously trying to keep control of himself. Alas, he failed in this, too. Scrambling to his feet, he dashed into the nearby garden enclosure and slammed the gate heavily behind him.

He didn't even have the satisfaction of a terran child, of hearing a loud slam behind him. The garden was designed as a place of peace and contemplation. The cushioned gate hinges automatically absorbed the shock of closing and snapped shut with a quiet click.

Spock remained standing quietly across the way, watching the direction his departing younger self had taken in disappearing among the thick vegetation. That green domesticated jungle had been his favorite place of hiding and solace as a boy.

This had been only one of many similar difficult moments in his childhood. It was not as painful to watch as it had been to live, but it was hard nonetheless.

"My apologies, visitor," came an unexpected voice—a deceptively quiet, unhurried, immensely powerful voice that he'd recognize anywhere. A voice that could impress whole worlds—or little boys. A second was sufficient time for him to compose himself. Then he turned, carefully keeping his expression open and receptive.

# VIII

Sarek of Vulcan stood opposite him, looking very much like the familiar picture Spock had seen earlier on the small triple screen in the command conference room. The only immediately obvious difference was that this living version had far less grey in his hair and eyebrows, far fewer age lines in his forehead and around the eyes.

A tall, broad-shouldered Vulcan he was, perhaps no athlete but in fine physical trim. He had sharply planed, strong features and deep-set eyes. Altogether an attractive man. An older, tauter, more severe version of Spock.

Spock calculated rapidly. His father should now be seventy-three standard years old, in the prime of Vulcan life. He wore the sandy-hued, neutral clothing Spock remembered so well. No loud shirts or bold prints for him! It was brightened only by a single spot of color, the adhesive badge of his office.

"I regret you were witness to that unfortunate display of emotion on the part of my son."

If there was any lingering hesitation in Spock's mind as to the identity of this man, that brief, so-typical phrase instantly dispelled it. This was Sarek, all right. Spock raised his hand in salute.

"In the family, all is silence. Especially the indiscretions of children. No more will be said of it. Live long and prosper, Sarek of Vulcan." The ambassador hesitated for a second before returning the salute.

"Peace and long life." Then he spoke uncertainly while

studying Spock with understandable puzzlement. "You are of my family?"

"A distant relative. My name is—" He paused. It wouldn't do to give an easily recognizable false name here. "—Selek. A humble cousin, descendant of T'pal and Sessek. I ... am journeying to the family shrine in Dycoon to honor our ancestors." There, that was a plausible reason for traveling the way he was. "Family is family, and I thought to give greeting to you on my passing."

Sarek nodded approvingly. "A pilgrimage, then?"

"Even so."

"You have a long way to go. Will you interrupt your journey to remain with us awhile, cousin?"

"I have already come quite a distance, and in good time," Spock murmured. "I have a little time to spare. I would be honored." He dipped his eyes, uncomfortably aware of Sarek's unwavering, intense stare. There was nothing he could do but try to ignore it.

"Is something wrong, cousin?" Spock asked. Sarek seemed to return from a region of far thoughts, formless musings.

"No, no. It was only that I seem to ... know you. To have met you before."

The best defense, Spock reflected, was a fast retreat through forward enemy positions.

"I, too," he countered, "have been struck by the physical resemblance between us. A common ancestor among our forefathers, no doubt."

"No doubt," agreed Sarek quietly. Then, as though suddenly remembering that to continue such a line of inquiry with a strange relative would have been impolite, "Well, come then. Allow me to welcome you to my home."

He turned and opened the beautifully carved gate behind them. Familiar, so familiar, was the interior of the house! Spock tried not to let his eyes stray overmuch. Everything was as he remembered it, everything fit so comfortably in his mind.

Except that most everything was just slightly smaller.

Sarek indicated a well-stuffed lounge of a type no longer made—there seemed to be few craftsmen left anymore—and then a nearby mechanical servitor. Spock eyed the quaint antique and tried not to feel superior. There were so many things he could tell his father, if only . . .

No. Impossible. Forget it.

"A place to rest and comfort yourself, cousin. Refreshments at hand, if you thirst. Excuse me. I shall return shortly. I have . . . an errand to perform. Meanwhile, my house is yours." He walked out of the room. Spock had a fair idea of the nature of his father's "errand."

Young Spock had buried himself against a shaggy wall of fur. He *might* have been crying, though it would have been difficult for an observer to tell. There was no sound.

The wall of fur filled out to north and south, completing the form of the youngster's pet sehlat, Ee-chiya. The sehlat looked rather like a cross between a lion and a giant panda, with a pair of downward projecting, ten-centimeter long fangs. It was fluffy, but not cute.

A temperamental sehlat would have been a poor choice of pet for a young human. But for the logical, never cruel or brutal Vulcan child, he was ideal—loving, intelligent and protective, as well as fiercely loyal.

This particular sehlat had a brown coat faded in spots to patches of pale beige. One of the worn, yellowed fangs was broken off at the tip, and there were other indications of the creature's advanced age.

Young Spock heard his father enter the garden, but he didn't look up from the massive flank.

"Spock . . ."

The boy slowly detached himself from the warm haven of Ee-chiya's furry side. He knew his father wouldn't repeat himself. He got slowly to his feet and shuffled over, presenting himself to his father in the traditional attitude of youthful respect—back straight, chin out, hands clasped firmly behind his back.

Sarek stood, looking down at his son for a moment, and then shook his head slightly, sadly. His voice was soft, but the words were not.

"Spock, being Vulcan means following disciplines and philosophies that are difficult and demanding of both mind and body. Do you understand?"

"Yes, Father."

"Your schoolwork has been disgraceful. You constantly display your emotions in public. You've even been seen fighting in the street, and your attitude in such conflicts is reported to have been somewhat less than experimentally martial." A hint of defiance crept into the youth's voice.

"Personal combat for a worthy cause is not dishonorable."

Inwardly, the reply pleased Sarek. However, the situation was serious. It could no longer be put off. This was not the time or place for him to express appreciation for such a sentiment.

"Brawling like a common deckhand off an alien freighter is not." Young Spock lowered his head.

"Yes, Father."

Sarek took a deep breath, paused, then continued more firmly.

"The time draws near when you will be forced to decide whether you'll follow Vulcan or human philosophies. Vulcan offers much. No war, no crime, with logic and reasoned guidance operating in place of raw emotion and unbridled passion. Once on the path you choose, you cannot turn back.

"Yes, Father."

Sarek lifted his gaze briefly, in a tiny display of disgust. That constant, meek "yes, Father" was beginning to annoy him. Perhaps he'd been, not too easy, but firm with the boy in the wrong ways.

Spock finished his drink and looked around the comfortable room. Still no sign of Sarek returning. He noticed old touches of Amanda's Earthwoman's influence—a cascade of brilliant blue flowers pouring over a flowerbox built into a wall. A dizzyingly colorful afghan tossed casually across a chair-back.

And the books—especially the books, on the shelves. Real books, to handle and read, not to be flashed and turned on by a dial on an electronic reader-viewer. He smiled inwardly. For those, at least, his childhood associates had envied him.

Impractical they might seem to many adult Vulcans, but they brought back a thrill of pride and memories to him. There was something about having the words there, in your hand. Any page, any chapter, at your personal beck and call—instead of having to plead for them through an electronic middleman.

He rose and walked to the large, open door that faced into part of the lush garden. Distantly, he could hear faint sounds of conversation between his father and his younger self, engaged in some deep discussion.

There had been many such discussions.

A soft, shocking voice made him whirl.

"I hope you were not disturbed by my son's behavior, cousin Selek."

Amanda stood there, even more beautiful than her picture, more lovely than any memory. Intelligent, gentle, and gracious. For the first time, he could admire her as a woman in the prime of her life, instead of as a boy seeing his mother.

And more than any other quality, he remembered, far more than beauty or wisdom—her constant understanding. Understanding for the ordeal of his childhood.

"No, my lady Amanda." He didn't even think the word "mother." This was one meeting he'd prepared for well and one mistake he was determined not to make. "Any child has much to learn. My young cousin has a more difficult road to travel than most others."

Now it was Amanda's turn to study him closely.

"You seem to understand him better than my husband."

Careful now! Sarek you could err with and cover up, but one slip with this woman and there would be trouble. She would not fool so easily.

"It is difficult for a father to bear less than perfection in his son. Spock will find a way, I suspect—his way." His mother looked anxious. He'd succeeded in diverting attention back to her son—from her son.

"I do hope so. I respect Vulcan and all its traditions, or I would not have married Sarek, but it's such a demanding life. It's hard enough on a young boy, without the added—complications my son must endure." The conversation was getting to be too painful for Spock.

"The boy appears to be of a certain age. He goes through the Kahs-wan ordeal soon, does he not?"

Amanda nodded. "Next month."

Visions of catastrophe, of a helix of mad time lines meeting in a common crazed center and dissolving into chaos, sprang into Spock's mind.

"Next . . . month?" He couldn't keep all the confusion and puzzlement out of his voice. "But tomorrow, tomorrow *is* the twentieth day of Tasmeen?" His mother looked up at him, disturbed a little by his controlled intensity.

"Yes, it is." That was reassuring, at least! The universe had not gone completely insane—though something was very, very wrong. "Is something the matter, cousin Selek?" Spock struggled to regain his composure.

"I've been traveling for quite awhile. I seem to have lost track of time."

". . . And that is all I have to say on the subject, for now," Sarek concluded. "Soon you will undergo your test of manhood, in the Kahs-wan. To survive for ten days without food, water, or weapons on Vulcan's Forge—as our human associates have so quaintly renamed the Sas-a-shar desert.

"It will demand more of you than anything else ever has. To fail once is not unusual, nor is it a disgrace—for others." Young Spock lowered his eyes again, studied the ground. But his father wasn't through.

"If you fail, there will be those who will nevertheless call you coward all your life." These last words rang like steel being hammered out on a Vulcanian forge of another type. That stentorian tone had been employed more than once for the glory of all Vulcan, in interstellar diplomacy. The tone was not softened for delivery from father to son.

"I do not expect you to fail."

Young Spock considered and looked up. "What if I do, father?"

Sarek could not admit to himself that there was anything so alien as emotion swirling through his mind.

"There is no need to ask that question. You will not disappoint me. You will not disappoint—yourself. Not if your heart and spirit are Vulcan."

He turned abruptly and walked back toward the house, leaving the youngster standing alone amid the silently watching blooms, the eloquent ferns. A few pebbles were lightly kicked by a small foot, a little earth disturbed.

Then he turned to the sehlat. The big mammal had dozed somnolently through the entire discussion, oblivious to the verbalizations of father and son. Now it stirred as his young master sat down beside him.

"Ee-chiya, what if I'm not a true Vulcan, like they say? What if Sepek and the others are right?"

The sehlat was not that intelligent. It did not understand. But it was sensitive to emotions. It snuffled and nudged nearer the boy, edging close in rough affection. Young Spock put his arms around as much of the massive neck as he could and hugged hard.

Spock maintained his own cover with near perfection throughout the rest of the day. He always managed to produce a plausible answer to any question Sarek or Amanda might pose, to turn awkward lines of inquiry neatly into other channels. It was a performance worthy of a diplomat's son.

He'd passed a pleasant, no, an ecstatic day, reliving the company of a younger mother and father, able to enjoy them as equals, to respond to them on entirely different yet equally gratifying levels.

He committed his one potentially serious error well after the sun had vanished below the horizon.

Sleep-time approached. As the guest, it was his place to mention such.

"I have had a long, full day, cousin Sarek, and your hospitality has been spoiling. I find myself more than ready for sleep." Sarek and Amanda both rose.

"Rest well, cousin," said Sarek. "We shall talk more tomorrow. I have enjoyed our evening immensely."

"It is the highlight of my journey, cousin Sarek," replied Spock, adding with an unseen smile, "perhaps I may remind you of it again some day."

Sarek looked at him oddly for a moment, then nodded politely. Amanda gestured, and Spock started to follow her towards the bedrooms. He almost turned in the direction of his own—young Spock's—room.

Fortunately, it was dark in the hallway and Amanda hadn't noticed the motion. He was barely able to recover before she glanced back at him.

She seemed willing to talk further at the door to the guest room, but he made further excuses of exhaustion. Too much close contact in the sometimes revealing dimness of evening might lead to unwanted questions.

He then attended to matters of Vulcan hygiene, enjoying once more the use of the interesting, old-fashioned washroom facilities. Then he returned to the guest room and turned on the single overhead light.

There was a lock on the door, but for a relative, a guest in another's house, to have bolted it would have been inexcusably bad manners. So, of course, would be the unannounced entrance of any member of the household. Still, he would have felt better with it bolted. He'd have to chance leaving it open. The single shuttered window he didn't worry about.

Sitting down on the edge of the bed he brought out his carry-bag. The little tricorder that came from it was far too modern and compact. The sleepwear he now wore was thirty years old, a simple garment of pale yellow worn like a loose toga.

One last time he considered locking the door, but discarded the idea. Instead he turned on the bed and put his back to it, shielding the potentially embarrassing tricorder with his body. And while recording, he kept his voice low. A passerby in the hall would have to strain to hear him and press an ear to the door to make any sense of what he said.

"Personal log, stardate 5373.9, subjective time.

"The time line seems to have changed once more, yet I cannot discover on thinking back anything I have done that might have affected it. My memory is quite clear regarding the actual day my cousin saved my life. That day is tomorrow." Then, as much to refresh his own memory as to provide information for future listeners:

"The Kahs-wan is an ancient rite of Vulcan's warrior days. When Vulcans turned to logic as the ruling element of their lives, they reasoned that it was necessary to maintain the old tests of strength and courage. Otherwise devotion to pure reason might make them grow weak and incapable of defending themselves from barbarians who might be less advanced mentally and socially.

"This, in itself, was of course a logical decision."

The house was very quiet. There was no pedestrian traffic on the surrounding pathways this late at night.

A door opened quietly in the rear of the house, and a very small, very young figure crept out. Young Spock was dressed in a desert soft-suit and boots. He closed the door carefully behind him and surveyed the area cautiously before moving any further out.

He took a couple of steps into the garden. There was a rustling sound from the shrubbery on his left and he froze.

A large, familiar shape lumbered into view—Ee-chiya, snuffling in the early morning air like an old man with a sinus condition. The boy shook his head, then held out a hand, palm up. The sehlat halted at the hand signal, but continued to puff and grunt. He certainly showed no sign of returning to sleep.

"No, Ee-chiya," he whispered. "This is my own test. I have to do it alone. Stay!" He moved away from the sehlat, heading for the garden gate.

Ee-chiya looked after him, considered this in his slow, patient mind, then turned and loped off after his young master.

Meanwhile, Spock had clicked off the compact tricorder and had carefully repacked it with other items deep in his carry-bag. His head dropped halfway to the headrest on the bed before he seemed to convulse. His head and upper torso came instantly erect. Realization hit him subtly— like a small nova.

Of course, he yelled to himself, I should have remembered! It wasn't the actual Kahs-wan ordeal his "cousin" had intervened in to save him!

Reaching for the carry-bag he made haste to unpack his clothes. It took only minutes to lay out the desert suit and boots, moving with as much speed as quiet would permit.

When the sun rose over the black mountains, it turned the hard-baked desert floor the color of molten lead. Ee-chiya still trailed close on young Spock's heels. They were headed for those same forbidding dark peaks. Under the circumstances and given the task he'd set himself, the peaks seemed as logical a place to prove himself as any other.

Quick physical collapse was an early threat of the real Kahs-wan. That was one test Spock no longer worried about. He strode along easily at an even pace, seemingly untired. Of course, all of his walking so far had been in the pleasant chill of night and the cool of early morning. Soon it would grow hot and the sun would pull moisture from him. That is, unless he elected to stop and find shelter for the day. He hadn't decided yet.

He refused to let such dismal possibilities intrude. Were it not for his anguished state of mind he could have enjoyed the hike. As for any unpleasantness that might lie ahead, he was determined not to let his spirits drop. The most important element in the Kahs-wan was mental.

Ee-chiya continued to mope along slightly behind. In his case it was not the *mental* aspect that was most important. The big animal was unused to such extended hiking. Eventually young Spock had to pause and wait for the sehlat to catch up.

Several long strides and his huge pet had done so. It promptly lay down on its belly, panting from the unaccustomed exertion and trying to catch its breath. Ee-chiya's spirit was willing, but the flesh was too old.

Besides, a sehlat's normal environment was the cool, high forests of the south. He managed well enough in his cool stall and in the thick shade of the garden at the house. But here, in open hot country his thick fur was a heavy burden. The rapidly rising heat would put a tremendous strain on the body of even a young, vigorous animal.

Young Spock stopped again and turned to face his pet squarely, hands on hips. His tone was gentle, but frustrated.

"Ee-chiya, go *home!* You are too old and too fat for this."

Ee-chiya leisurely examined this statement from his position on the warming sands. Then he put his great head down on his forepaws and assumed an air of patient dignity. Young Spock shook his head determinedly.

"Huh-uh, that's how you always get your way with father. It won't work with me. Go home, Ee-chiya."

The sehlat took no notice. He seemed quite prepared to spend the rest of his existence on this spot. It was clear to young Spock that the only way the beast would return home would be while trailing its master.

And he had a great deal to accomplish before that return journey could take place. He sighed, shrugged, and lifted his shoulders in a very human gesture that said, "I've done what I can." Then he turned and started off towards the high range at the same steady pace he'd maintained since leaving home.

Ee-chiya waited only a few seconds. Then he lurched to his feet and shuffled off to join his master.

After a while, another, taller figure reached the same spot. It paused to examine the depression left in the sand and soft gravel by Ee-chiya's relaxing bulk. A light breeze off distant desert plains swept sand and twigs into miniature dust demons, threatening manifestations of Vulcan's turbulent atmosphere.

He pulled out the tricorder as he resumed his walk. The trail of young Spock was clear enough, that of the sehlat was unmistakable.

"Personal log—the boy Spock should be moving toward the Arlanga mountains. He . . . ," Spock hesitated, "I . . . had much to prove to myself. The personal ordeal, I now remember, on which I embarked was meant to determine the course my life would take. Many things are coming back to me now, as I retrace my steps of thirty years past and as I become more familiar with this time of my youth."

Sarek was just entering the garden. Amanda spotted him and left the shady seat to rush into his arms. She was calmer, more controlled than most terran women would have been in a similar situation. But to one of her Vulcan neighbors, she would have appeared almost hysterical.

"Sarek, I've looked everywhere. Our son and the guest are gone."

"And Ee-chiya?" asked Sarek calmly. Amanda frowned. She didn't know what she'd expected him to say, but that was not it.

"Ee-chiya?"

"He would go with our son," Sarek noted, "as he always does."

"I haven't seen him, now that you mention it, Sarek."

Sarek nodded. "I feel more secure knowing that. Ee-chiya's getting old, but it will be difficult for the boy to get into any serious trouble with the sehlat around. You're certain he's with the stranger?" Amanda looked uncertain.

"I don't know, really. Spock's not anywhere in the neighborhood—I've checked—and it's not like him to go off any distance without telling me. I don't know what else to think."

"This cousin," mused Sarek, "he puzzles me. Something very odd about him. I sometimes think I can see it, and then it suddenly eludes me again." Amanda gave an anxious start.

"You don't think he'd harm Spock?"

"I don't know what to think, Amanda. The man claims to be a relative and is friendly enough, yet there is this lingering strangeness about him that all his good-naturedness cannot conceal. However, I will take no chances. I shall notify the proper authorities immediately to watch out for either of them."

Amanda bit her lip. That was the only logical thing to do.

The desert ended abruptly in the first rugged ramparts of the mountains. Spock knelt to study the fresh trail of boy and sehlat, then rose and began his first real climb. The morning sun exceeded his rate of ascent.

The various formations he passed as he moved higher into the foothills were of igneous rock, stark and weirdly shaped. Not from wind erosion, but by the primeval forces of Vulcan itself. This was an area of geologically recent plutonic activity.

Once the ground turned upward his path became more difficult. Spock climbed slowly and carefully.

Something sounded in the air, distant. He stopped climbing and turned his head to listen. Nothing.

Several steps later he heard it again and this time it was unmistakable and much louder. A sound ... no, there were two sounds, separate and distinct. One was a deep, grinding snarl, the other the scream of an animal with a much higher-pitched voicebox.

The sounds conveyed anger and fury rather than fear. He began climbing faster. Each boulder seemed intent only on slowing his progress, every small fissure designed to catch and trip him.

Then he was running along a channel out through naked rock. The old watercourse twisted and turned before finally opening into a broad natural amphitheater.

On the far side young Spock was scrambling for safety, trying to stay behind protective rocks and at the same time gain height. The le-matya swung at him with venomous claws. They barely missed a trailing leg, digging shallow gouges in the soft stone. As young Spock dodged behind another boulder the le-matya screamed in frustration.

It was built like a terran mountain lion, but huge. The nearly impenetrable leathery-grey hide was more reptilian than mammalian, as was the poison in its claws. Again the high-pitched scream sounded, like the sound of metal rubbing on metal at high speed, grating from the depths of that awful gullet.

The youngster moved higher and reached for a handhold. Instead of a handhold he found himself confronted by a sheer wall of shining black obsidian. It was no more than three meters high—not much of a barrier. But there was no way up it and no way around. It might as well have been three thousand.

He turned his back to the volcanic glass and awaited the le-matya's charge. If he could dodge the first swipe of the monster's claws, he might be able to slip past on that side before it could swing again. The le-matya snarled and drew back a paw for a last, final blow.

It was never delivered.

An aging Ee-chiya struck the le-matya like a runaway warp-drive, rolling it over completely on the high ledge. The heavy, square head, neither cuddly nor benign now, bit quickly and with surprising speed. Yellowing old teeth made a deep double slash in the le-matya's flank.

Spitting and squalling, the carnivore twisted free, clawing at the sehlat. Ee-chiya darted out of the way and threw a blow with one massive paw that barely missed crushing the le-matya's skull. The half-reptile glared and leaped at the sehlat with both sets of claws extended. Ee-chiya dodged that multiple death and in doing so lost his balance.

Both animals clashed together, off stride and on crumbling, uncertain footing. There was a moment's pause while they overbalanced. Then, locked in each other's grips, they tumbled over and over, clawing and biting, down the short slope. Ee-chiya's low, rhythmic snarls boomed in counterpoint to the le-matya's high-pitched, hysterical screams.

Spock hesitated only a moment. To challange a le-matya unarmed was certain death. But for a while, the sehlat had it fully occupied. Maybe, just maybe . . .

He ran straight for the massive collage of fighting flesh. Young Spock saw him coming. But the sudden unexpected appearance of his cousin generated only mild concern. He was too worried about Ee-chiya.

The sehlat had managed to bury his fangs in the le-matya's thick hide. Powerful teeth failed to do much damage. His jaw muscles were too old and weak. There wasn't even much blood oozing from that armored skin. But the considerable bulk of the sehlat kept the writhing, spinning le-matya continuously off-balance.

It never saw Spock moving close by, eyeing it, waiting for a chance. The le-matya dug in and started to roll Ee-chiya over on his back preparatory to a killing strike. As the armored spine came up Spock saw his opening, ran, made the short leap. He landed firmly on the carnivore's back.

Incensed at the sudden new weight on its shoulders the le-matya exploded in frenzied anger. It jerked and twisted, trying to buck Spock off. Ee-chiya skidded back out of the way as the le-matya frantically tried to deal with this tiny but unrelenting tormentor. It screamed again and again.

By simply lying still and rolling over it could easily have dislodged Spock. But a le-matya, while long on ferocity and strength, was notably deficient in matters mental. So it did not roll over. Instead it kept spinning in circles and leaping high in the air, trying to bite at the thing on its back. It had no luck.

Making a vise of his thighs and digging one hand into loose, flying hair, Spock leaned forward along the smooth neck and felt for the certain special joining on the animal's neck. If it suddenly decided to roll over, or jump back first against a boulder . . . He couldn't hold on indefinitely, and to let go now was an easy way of committing suicide.

There! That should be the place. Small but powerful fingers touched, moved.

The le-matya gave a long, drawn-out shudder. As the wild eyes closed it sank unconscious to the earth. Now the muscular form started to roll over on its side, but Spock was not worried as he jumped clear.

Turning, he glanced up the slope, but the boy was already down off the dark rocks and running towards the sehlat.

Ee-chiya was getting slowly to his feet when young Spock reached him. He threw his arms around the big animal's neck. The slight boyish shape had no effect on the huge furry mass. It shook itself, a long rolling oscillation that commenced at the nose and fluttered back to the short tail.

It seemed that his pet was unharmed, merely out of breath.

"Ee-chiya," muttered the youth, unable to enjoy the emotional release of crying. "Good boy, good old boy!"

Forgotten, but not upset by the neglect, Spock dusted himself off and walked over to the two companions. He'd bruised his thighs with the shifting, frictioning grip he'd held on the le-matya's back, and there was a possibility of a broken toe, but otherwise he was intact. He cleared his throat.

"I suggest we move away from this area before the le-matya regains consciousness. I do not think it will follow us, now, but it would be better not to tempt it."

"True," replied the boy, then, "thank you for helping me and Ee-chiya."

"It was only my duty, Spock," the elder version of himself told the younger. The reply held a slight hint of reproof.

"Mother says you should always say 'you're welcome.'"

That caught Spock a little off guard. There was an awkward silence. Some sort of reply seemed called for.

"The lady Amanda is noted for her graciousness."

The youngster looked over at the motionless le-matya, a threatening shape even while unconscious, then back up at his cousin. He continued to stroke Ee-chiya's fur.

"Do you think I'll ever be able to do that neck pinch as well as you, cousin Selek?"

"I dare say you will," admitted Spock drily. "Come now. Let us leave this place."

They moved off, heading up the slope. A little while later they had circled the far curve of the amphitheater and were heading deeper into the mountains.

Neither of them noticed the occasional shiver that passed through the sehlat's body. Nor could they see inside to learn that the big animal was moving with increasing difficulty.

They'd entered an area where huge boulders and unworn volcanic rock had begun to mix with soil. The first deciduous trees grew here, marching down in friendly ranks from the wetter high plateau. Young Spock spoke again, his voice full of open childish curiosity.

"You followed me—why?"

For a quick moment Spock felt that he didn't have to be as careful as he'd had to be with his mother and father. But he paused before replying. Overconfidence might be his biggest danger. After all, his verbal inquisitor, though young, had an undeniably brilliant mind.

"I suspected you might attempt something of this sort. I sensed your worry about the Kahs-wan. Such an expedition seemed a very natural gesture." Young Spock looked up at him.

"I had to see if I could do it. A personal test first, a test for me and no one else. I *cannot* fail!"

"That is your father's desire?"

The boy spoke slowly, choosing his words with care.

"Yes, and my mother's. They ... they confuse me, sometimes. Father wants me to do things his way, and when I ask her, Mother says that I should. But then she goes and—" He stopped and looked away from Spock, suddenly embarrassed over what he was about to confess.

Remembering, Spock continued the thought himself. "She's a human woman with strong emotions and sensitivities." He kicked at a loose pebble, unaware that he was repeating a gesture performed several times by his younger self the previous day.

"She embarrasses you when she displays those traits. And you are afraid when you see them in yourself, because of what your father wishes."

"How ... how did you know?" young Spock murmured, quietly amazed. Uh-oh—it took Spock some fast thinking to find a way around that one.

"There is also some human blood in my family line, Spock." Then he added, taking some of the solemnity off the conversation, "It is not fatal."

"What you do not yet understand, Spock," the first officer of the *Enterprise* continued, "is that Vulcans do not *lack* emotion. This is an all too common misconception— among many Vulcans as well as among other races. It is merely that ours are controlled, kept in check. This adherence to principles of logic offers a serenity that others— excepting certain theological and philosophical orders— rarely experience in full."

"We have emotions, you see, so that is nothing to be ashamed of. It is as natural as having a sense of sight, or touch. But we deal firmly with them and do not let them control us. Nor are humans, like your mother, wholly ruled by their emotions. Instead, they must walk an uneasy, nerve-wracking tight-rope between the Vulcan principles of logic and reason and the—"

He would have said more—suddenly there were so many things he wanted to say to this boy—but they were interrupted by a low moan. It came from behind them.

Startled, they both turned. Ee-chiya was no longer right behind them. Instead he stood far back, half-leaning against a broken cliff-face. He showed no sign of moving toward them. They ran to the sehlat's side.

Up close, they could now see that the huge animal was swaying unsteadily on his feet. By the time they reached him he'd sunk slowly to the ground, his eyes glazed and dim.

"Ee-chiya!" young Spock shouted, completely forgetting Spock's recent lecture on logic and emotion. The science officer made an efficient, rapid examination of the distressed animal. If he could only remember the details of his own childhood, he'd know exactly what was the matter! He'd been through this experience once before—or had he? Everything was so vague.

The time was so distant, so insubstantial, so . . .

Nonsense, he told himself. The past was now—and it was very real.

Then he found what he was looking for—but didn't expect to find. Puzzled, he stared at it until he grew aware of young Spock's anxious gaze.

"It appears that the le-matya grazed him with a claw, here. A slight wound, not too deep. But that does not matter much, not with a le-matya. It should not have happened. I don't seem to recall—"

The boy interrupted. "Is he dying?"

Spock considered. When he finally replied it was with a double pain. Pain for himself, pain for what he must say.

"Yes."

The youngster looked stricken. He stared down at the rapidly weakening, moaning sehlat.

Spock walked away a few steps, his thoughts spinning. For the second time something completely unexpected had happened. Try as he might, he couldn't remember anything like this taking place before.

But musing on the perversity of the time vortex would do no good at all. The animal was dying. He would be dead already, only the strike had been a shallow one. So Ee-chiya had not received a normal dose of venom. There might be a chance.

But the boy's pet—his pet—would die for certain unless they could bring a healer here, and soon. He told young Spock as much, making no effort to sugarcoat the news.

"We cannot get him back to the city to a healer. He is too large to move without special equipment."

"Then what," and young Spock's tone was agonized, "can we *do*? There must be something."

"You are a Vulcan. What would be the logical thing to do?" The boy thought, looked up brightly.

"I have medicines in my desert kit. Can . . . ?" Spock shook his head slowly.

"Even if by some chance you have a proper medication, there could not possibly be a large enough dose for an animal the size of Ee-chiya. Try again."

The youthful brow twisted with concentration, the mouth grimaced with the strain of furious thought. He looked up again.

"I can bring a *healer* here."

"It is a long journey back across the desert," Spock warned. "There are many dangers. And it will be night again soon. I will go." But his youthful self stood up, his voice defiant, determined.

"No. He is my pet. It is my duty. No one else can do this for me. But, will you stay with him?"

Spock considered, trying to keep events sorted out. If this had actually happened before, then his younger self should succeed in the journey. If it hadn't already occurred, and this was yet another variant in the time line, he might be risking his own life in *all* time lines by letting the boy go. Then he remembered the uncertainties of his early adolescence, the constant burning desire to prove himself again and again. He nodded his acquiescence, but reluctantly.

Young Spock took off immediately, disappearing over the rolling, heat-warped horizon in the direction of ShiKahr. Once the boy was out of sight, Spock relaxed and regarded the dying sun. It turned the desert floor to deep purples and threw maroon shadows in the lee of small dunes.

He reached out and idly stroked the massive head of the sehlat. The big fellow looked up at him trustingly. But it was also confused. That was no surprise. This was the first time it had gotten a close whiff of Spock. Obviously this tall stranger was not his young master.

And yet—smell and to a small extent sight, said otherwise. It was very puzzling.

"This did not happen before, I am sure of it," Spock said to him, ruffling the warm fur behind an ear. "My life's decision was made without the sacrifice of yours, old friend."

Ee-chiya moaned softly and stayed calm under Spock's ministering hands.

"I know there is pain. I can help a little. Sleep now."

He reached over and moved both hands on the sehlat's neck, probing. Then he made a motion similar to, and yet unlike, the thing he had done to the le-matya. The great eyes closed all the way and the entire massive body seemed to slump.

Spock sat back and watched the desert. Absently, gently, he continued to stroke the now supine head. Kirk would have found the present tableau incongruous. Doubtless Dr. McCoy would have seen in it opportunities to apply his own particular brand of humor.

But to Amanda or Sarek, the pose would have looked entirely natural and very very much in character.

It grew dark rapidly and soon young Spock had to depend on his natural, well-developed night vision. Vulcan had no moon.

He moved at a fast jog across the black, shadowed landscape. His eyes rarely took note of dim shapes and distant moving objects. They stayed fixed on the ground in front of him. A few small nocturnal animals observed the passage of the slim, ghostly shape. They scurried instinctively for the safety of their burrows.

Once, the predatory shriek of a night-hunting le-matya cut the air. It was distant, and young Spock didn't break his stride. But he did look back over his shoulder. And in not looking ahead, he failed to see the coil of dark vines half-buried in the sand.

Another step—the vines suddenly uncoiled, snapping out like a dozen whips and grabbing at his legs. He made a half-running, half-standing leap that would have done credit to any athlete in his age class and fairly flew over the powerful thin tentacles.

There was a sharp, popping sound. One convulsing, clutching coil had just missed his ankle and snapped instead against the heel of his left boot. He continued on, resolving to keep his eyes on the rough gravel and sand immediately in front of him even if a le-matya screamed right in his ear.

The writhing unthinking vines of the carnivorous *d'mallu* did not ponder on the near miss. They merely recoiled and reset as the plant—with the inherent patience of all growing things—arranged itself once more to wait for less elusive prey.

There was a peculiar emblem on the door, cut into the highly varnished yellow wood and inlaid with shiny metal. Below this an odd-shaped plaque, functional as well as decorative, was also recessed in the wood.

A soft, tinkling clash—wind playing with distant temple bells. It stopped, started again as young Spock shoved insistently against the plaque.

It seemed ages passed before the door finally opened. A tall, middle-aged Vulcan appeared, dressed in a togalike night garment. This toga was red with garish blue stripes. A private expression of a publicly prosaic physician.

The elder eyed Spock with evident displeasure. He was not in the mood for idle chitchat.

"The hour is late. I trust your errand is urgent?"

"Yes—," young Spock panted, trying to catch his breath and speak at the same time. "Most urgent, Healer. My sehlat fought a le-matya in the foothills. He suffered a small wound. The poison of the le-matya's claws is working in him now. Please—" The carefully maintained, even tone began to crack. "You must come with me. He needs your knowledge!"

The healer considered, studying his late-night caller. The dim light at the door made recognition difficult, but not impossible.

"You are Spock, son of Sarek, are you not?"

"Yes, Healer." The physician nodded in satisfaction.

"I have heard of you. You have a tendency toward what humans call 'practical jokes.' "

The youth nodded knowingly. He'd expected something like this. Vulcan gossip reached far and lasted long.

"It's true, I did that two years ago, and did not repeat it. Healer, I would not call you out at such an hour if it were not deathly serious. You have heard several things about me, it seems. Have you ever heard the son of Sarek called a liar?"

The healer's tone softened. Such direct challenge from one so young could only be admired.

"No. That has never been said." A quick glance at the boy's disheveled clothes and flushed face brought him to a decision.

"Very well. Wait here and I will gather my things."

Young Spock called after him as he disappeared into the house.

"Healer, please hurry!" Inwardly, he was relieved. He'd delivered himself and his message so quickly, so urgently, that the healer had not thought to ask a most obvious question.

What was a young lad of seven doing in the black mountains with his sehlat in the middle of the night, and why had he come alone to get help?

Spock was not ready to waste time on embarrassing explanations.

It was wondrous strange to be sitting alone at night with a dying figure out of one's old childhood, instead of in the commander's cabin on the *Enterprise*.

The sehlat moaned softly, conscious once again. A quiver of pain ran down its flanks. Inside Spock's belly something tightened. There was nothing more he could do for the suffering animal. To put it under again might prove fatal in itself, given the advanced state of weakness of the creature's systems.

There was another soft moan. At first he ignored it. Then he rose and stared into the night. The moan was still distant, but growing rapidly louder. It had not come from the sehlat.

It was a thick purr now, rough and mechanical. He

scanned the dark horizon wishing, wishing for a battery of portable lights from the starship. But the *Enterprise* had not even been built yet. He didn't have so much as a flare.

It was needed. Silhouetted against the night sky, he saw the source of the sound. A desert flier, a streamlined version of the standard city skimmer. Low and rakish, but practical, built for emergency bursts of speed.

An ordinary citizen would not rate such an expensive, compact craft. Logically, he had no need of it. It was also bigger than the average skimmer, big enough to carry several passengers. There were only two figures in it.

As the craft drifted closer he recognized his younger self and another, older man. That could only be the healer young Spock had gone to find.

The skimmer came close. It whined to a halt and hovered a meter or so off the ground. The rocks where he waited with Ee-chiya were jagged and close together, so the skimmer pilot had settled down in the nearest flat space. It raised a cloud of sand and dust before the older Vulcan cut its power.

He climbed out, and young Spock began to lead him up into the rocks. Spock turned and walked back to stand next to the heaving bulk of the sehlat. He stroked the head, scratched it behind weakly fluttering ears.

"It will not be long now, old friend."

A moment later young Spock and the healer appeared, scrambling over the last rise. They moved to join him.

The healer took only the briefest of looks at the long scratch where the le-matya's claws had struck. Then he removed several compact medical sensors from his carrycase and began a thorough examination of the stricken animal.

Spock stood and placed a hand on the youngster's shoulder. From the first there had been no shock at the sight of his younger self. He'd been well prepared for that. But this first actual physical contact brought home the alienness of the situation in a way that mere sight never could.

The full, true incredibility of it slammed home for the first time. Under his hand the boyish shoulder stirred. Spock felt a need to mumble something, anything.

"You made the desert crossing most efficiently, Spock. And at night too. I have a hunch—call it a preliminary evaluation based on sound initial observations—that you will not fail your father in the Kahs-wan." Young Spock didn't look up at him, instead kept his gaze focused on the sehlat and the healer.

"I wanted only to help Ee-chiya. He was my father's before he was mine. I didn't want him to come with me, but he wouldn't stay behind. To lose him—" Spock interrupted as gently as possible.

"A Vulcan would face such a loss without tears."

*"How?"* Controlled or not, there was a universe of emotion packed into that one word, that single desperate exclamation.

"By understanding that every life comes to an end when—when time demands it. Believe me, Spock, when I say that the demands of time are not to be argued with. Loss of life is to be mourned, true, but only if that life was wasted.

"Such was not the case with Ee-chiya."

The healer looked up from the sehlat. He had to hunt a moment before locating them in the dark.

"Spock?" The youngster turned. So, automatically, did the older Spock. The boy glanced up at him curiously, but there were other things on his mind. He dismissed the incident as he moved closer to the healer. Spock followed, thankful that the healer had not witnessed the lapse in his meticulous masquerade.

"Yes, sir?" The sehlat was moaning louder and continuously now. The healer glanced down at the animal and shook his head slowly.

"It has been too long, I fear, and the scratch was deep enough. No known antidote can save his life." The boy stood silently in the dark, contemplative.

"Is there nothing you can do?"

"To save him, nothing. But I can prolong his life— though he will always be in pain. Or . . . I can release him from life. In this I will need your decision. He is your pet." The healer did not look up at him.

Alien, unchildish thoughts vied for attention within young Spock's mind. He turned away from the two adults

so they could not see the effort he was putting into his answer—or the anguish that might be visible.

Spock waited several minutes, then moved up quietly to
stand behind the boy. He put his hand on the small shoulder once more. This time there was no shock, no sense of
unnaturalness. For the first time, he truly was Selek, the
wise cousin. Young Spock glanced up at him, then back
down at Ee-chiya. When he spoke it was in a flat,
mechanical voice, to the healer.

"Release him. It is fitting he dies as he lived—with peace
and dignity."

The healer nodded expressionlessly and reached into his
case. He withdrew a small tube whose size and looks belied its effectiveness. There were only three controls on
it—two tiny dials and a button at one end.

He adjusted the settings. Young Spock watched for another moment, then walked over and knelt beside the
sehlat. He sat down on the hard ground and took the massive head in his lap.

Ee-chiya stared up at him and burrowed himself
deeper, closer to the boy. There was an ethereal, minute
hiss as though from a tiny spray. Young Spock's face remained unchanged, emotionless—Vulcan!

"I regret that my actions troubled you in any way, Father," young Spock said, "but I am convinced my actions
were necessary." Sarek blinked in the strong light pouring
in through the garden window as he studied his son.

There was something in the youth's attitude and speech
pattern that the elder Vulcan had not detected before. In
fact, both seemed somehow rather like . . . he chanced a
quick and hopefully unnoticed glance towards his odd
cousin, standing impassively by a far bookcase.

Spock was studiously examining an ancient terran
book. It happened to be a fantasy, a childhood favorite of
his by a terran with an odd name. Sarek could not see the
title and it probably wouldn't have set any thoughts going
in his head anyway. The paper books were Amanda's
province. His mother, however, might have made something of the coincidence, but she was too relieved to notice
much of anything but her son just now.

Sarek turned back to the boy.

"I hope you can explain *why* it was necessary. Your mother and I were . . . worried."

"There was a decision to be made," said young Spock firmly. "A direction for my life had to be chosen—and before the artificiality of the Kahs-wan. I chose—Vulcan."

On the other side of the room, Amanda turned away briefly in her chair, fighting off tears. She felt a slight sense of loss, common to all mothers at those strange, off-center times when they realize their child is growing up. Her son had elected to follow the more difficult path.

Sarek exhibited no outward reaction to this announcement—but he was naturally pleased. Of course, it would be unthinkable to show it, or to smile. He nodded solemnly.

"It is well. You have comported yourself with honor." He paused. "We will see to it that Ee-chiya is brought home from the mountains."

"Thank you, Father." Young Spock shuffled his feet impatiently. "If you will excuse me now, I have some business to attend to."

"Business?" queried Sarek suspiciously.

"With some schoolmates. A demonstration of the Vulcan neck pinch. Our cousin taught me." He nodded by way of excusing himself and left the room.

When he'd departed, Spock replaced the friendly old tome in its slot on the shelf and moved towards Sarek and Amanda.

"I, too, must beg to be excused. I must make my farewells now. Your hospitality has been most kind, more than you can know. But I must journey on. Already I have spent too much . . ." he paused and almost, *almost* grinned, "too much time here."

"Just enough time," said Sarek gratefully. "You saved my son's life. There is no way I can ever repay you for that." Spock interrupted him smoothly, his voice turning serious.

"Try to understand your son, Sarek of Vulcan. His troubles, his confusion, his battles with his emotions. That will be repayment enough."

"An odd and intimate request from a stranger, but I

will honor it. I am bound to honor it. If you ever pass this
way again, or if there is anything I can ever do for you—
all that I have is yours."

"I should like to, but I fear that circumstance will dic-
tate that I not retrace this path again." This was becoming
too painful. It was time to leave. He raised his hand in
salute. "Peace and long life, cousin."

"Peace and long life," saluted his mother and father in
return. "Long life and prosper, cousin."

He didn't look back as he left the garden gate and started
down the path leading back toward the desert. But he
could feel their curious eyes on his back, watching,
watching . . .

He remembered now that his parents had never men-
tioned a cousin Selek. He smiled inwardly. Even so, he
understood now why he had never forgotten that remarkable individual . . .

James T. Kirk paced nervously back and forth in front
of the Time Gate. He was alone on the rocky platform in
front of the Guardian of Forever.

Unresolvable shapes drifted across the center of the
time portal, cloaking unknown mysteries, enigmatic pasts.
Suddenly he stopped pacing and stared at the rippling
mists. They began to slow, to organize and coalesce into a
definite pattern. The Gate was activating.

It was confirmed a second later as a deep, now familiar
rumble issued from some still indeterminate locale.

"THE TRAVELER IS RETURNING."

Kirk studied the Gate with painful expectation. At first
there was nothing. He began to worry. Then, in the distance, a transparent flowing form seemed to jump towards
him. It was solidifying as it came through the Gate.

A familiar lanky frame, clad in the attire of another
world's bygone days, stepped out and shook hands with
him. Spock didn't say anything—but Kirk had had
enough experience reading barely noticeable Vulcan expressions to tell that the trip hadn't been a total disaster.

Spock went immediately to his waiting pile of normal
clothing. Off came the worn soft-suit and tight boots,

swapped for the daytime uniform of a Starfleet commander.

"I sent the others up to the ship," Kirk volunteered in response to the unasked question. He nodded in the direction of the again blurred time portal. "What happened in there? You were only gone twenty-four minutes ... subjective time."

"Nothing different happened, nothing unexpected, Captain." He paused. "Oh, one small thing was changed, nothing vital. A pet died."

Kirk looked relieved. "A pet? Well, that wouldn't mean much in the course of time."

"It might," Spock replied, "to some—"

Kirk eyed his first officer more closely as he swapped Vulcan carry-bag for utility belt, communicator, and other modern necessities. Kirk hesitated, decided to ask no further questions—for now. There were more important ones to be answered. He flipped open his communicator.

"*Enterprise* ... this is the captain. We're moving away from the Guardian. There'll be two to beam up."

"Aye, sir," came Engineer Scott's reply.

A moment later both men stood still as a luminescent glow enveloped them and turned them into pieces of sun.

This state was quickly reversed in the main transporter room of the starship. Both Kirk and Spock held their positions, however, after rematerializing—Kirk uncertain, Spock apprehensive.

"Well, well, well!" Dr. McCoy stepped into view from behind the transporter console as Scott concluded final shutdown. The doctor looked at them and nodded knowingly, his tone as irascible as ever.

"So you two finally decided to end your vacation. While you've been running all over creation, I've been stuck performing semiannual crew physicals. You two are the last ones." Captain and commander exchanged glances, each certain he was more relieved than the other.

"Welcome aboard, Mr. Spock," said Kirk. McCoy moved closer, shepherding them out of the alcove and toward the elevator.

"Never mind the chitchat. I've got the mediscanners all set up for a Vulcan. I have to recalibrate every time I run a check on you, Spock." He made it sound like the biggest job since the hammering out of the Federation-Klingon peace treaty.

"Dr. McCoy," said Spock, moving towards the closed doors, "you do not know the half of your good fortune. If things were only slightly different you might have to re-calibrate for, say, an Andorian."

He and Kirk activated the call switch simultaneously.

"What's that supposed to mean?" McCoy inquired. When neither man replied. "If that's supposed to be a joke, I have to remind you that Vulcans don't tell jokes." He followed them into the waiting elevator.

"Times change, Doctor," suggested Spock meaningfully, "times change."

McCoy grunted, sensing something more than mere argument in the first officer's voice.

"Just give me time enough for a physical, that's all."

"All the time in the world, Doctor." Kirk grinned as McCoy hit the necessary button and they began to descend to lower levels.

It wasn't often he enjoyed something as much as that simple elevator ride.

# PART III

# ONE OF OUR PLANETS IS MISSING

(Adapted from a script by Marc Daniels)

# IX

Precisely two and a quarter ship-days after leaving the Time Planet the crew of the *Enterprise* received a general emergency call. There were undoubtedly rarer things in the universe than general emergency calls—but not many.

"What I'd like to know," Kirk inquired of no one in particular, from his seat in the bridge command chair, "was why someone didn't notice and chart this thing before it slipped into inhabited Federation space?"

Lt. Arex was seated next to Sulu at the helm-computer. Now he lifted all three arms in a popular human gesture and swiveled his thin neck so that he was facing the captain. Bright, intelligent eyes stared out from under projecting ridges of bone.

"*Quien sabe?* Who knows, Captain?"

Uhura's reaction was more reasoned. "Maybe no one thought it worth an emergency alert, Captain, until it did move so deep into Federation territory. It hasn't made any aggressive moves. Why should it attract much attention while in free space?"

"Even given its benign nature, Lieutenant—something of which we have as yet no proof," countered Spock, "the fact that a cosmic cloud of this size and density—not to mention its other peculiar characteristics—has never been observed before should have been sufficient to pique the interest of at least a couple of astronomers. I cannot help but wonder if there are other reasons why it was not detected."

Kirk grunted. They'd been examining and reexamining

these same arguments ever since the call had been received. He didn't make a point of it, but he was upset. They'd been returning to starbase from the planet of the time vortex when the call had diverted them. R&R for the crew, not to mention needed ship-servicing, had to be postponed yet again.

"Just our usual luck—the *Enterprise* being the only starship of any size in the phenomenon's vicinity. Sometimes I get the feeling Starfleet Command picks on us."

"I suspect, Captain," Spock suggested, "that if we were to perform below expectations a few times, Starfleet would be in less of a hurry to select us for such tasks."

"Don't tempt me, Mr. Spock."

"I was not tempting you, Captain. I was merely proposing an alternative mode of operation with an eye toward alleviating your apparent discomfort at being so often chosen by Starfleet Command for such—"

"Oh, never mind, Mr. Spock." If he thought Spock was capable of ironic humor, he'd have suspected that—no, ridiculous.

"Mr. Sulu, let's see the grid."

"Yes, sir." Sulu's hands moved over the complex navigation console. A brilliant star-chart appeared on the main viewscreen. The overlying grid network permitted fast, crude calculation of speed and distances. Kirk's interest was on the Pallas XIV system. The exaggerated diagram showed close to one side of the moving white dot that was the *Enterprise*.

Three planets—Bezaride, Mantilles, and Alondra, plus a fair-sized asteroid belt—extended outward from Pallas I and II. All were small, inner-system type worlds. There were no gas giants.

The system revolved around a double star. Double-star systems were far from unusual, but those with planets were. And those with inhabited worlds were very much so. The Pallas system was very carefully studied before settlement was recommended. Not that Pallas II—Mantilles —was not a hospitable world. Quite the contrary. But Federation authorities wanted to make, well, double certain that the twin-star system was stable enough to support Mantillian life for at least a minimal period of time. Say, four or five hundred million years.

In addition to being blessed with two shadows per person, Mantillians enjoyed the notoriety of being the most remote inhabited world of consequence in the entire Federation. And while the planet was now safely populated and well beyond the initial stages of colonization, the Mantillians still liked to think of themselves as pioneers—their backs to the populous Federation and galactic center, their faces turned to the beckoning gulfs of intergalactic space.

They were a proud, self-reliant people. But the sudden appearance of this strange cloud had made them nervous. So the Mantillian government had shouted loud enough for Starfleet Command to hear, and Starfleet Command had shouted for the *Enterprise*.

And Kirk—Kirk could only shout at the gods of coincidence and bad timing. At least they didn't shout back, they only snickered.

He sighed. They were here. Find out what the thing was, reassure the Mantillians, and head for starbase once again—with closed channels this time, maybe.

"Mr. Sulu, let's have some timings." The helmsman's reply was quick and crisp.

"We will intercept the cloud in the vicinity of Pallas III—Alondra. The outermost planet, sir. It is not inhabited. There are only a few automatic scientific stations." Spock looked up from his hooded viewer at the computer-library console.

"Also, Captain, I might add that we are now approaching sensor range of the cloud."

"Initial readings, Mr. Spock? Starfleet wasn't very specific. I kind of got the impression they expected us to dig out our own information." He tried to show some interest as Spock looked back into his viewer and adjusted controls. Probably the cloud was a loose piece of nebula, a relatively harmless collection of thin cosmic gases.

Spock's report changed all that. There was nothing ordinary about *this* cloud.

"It is an irregular shape with shifting, undefined boundaries, Captain. On the mean, I would estimate some eight hundred thousand kilometers across and perhaps half that in depth. And it is quite dense." The soft-spoken Arex looked up from his seat at the helm and whistled, impressed.

"Immense! Twice the diameters of Sol III's three biggest gas giants combined!"

"We're all well grounded in basic astronomy, Lt. Arex," said Kirk drily. "Put up our present position, please."

Arex, looking slightly downcast, went to work at the console. "Yes, Captain."

Inwardly, Kirk chastised himself. There was really no call for coming down on Arex like that. He was only expressing a sense of awe and wonder at the sight of the peculiar intruder, a feeling everyone else probably shared. It was a liberty Kirk couldn't permit himself. Captains weren't supposed to be awed.

Anyway, it wasn't the thing's size that had suddenly worried him. It was Spock's information that the cloud was "quite dense." Sizewise it was small stuff compared to even a little nebula. But if the gas was thick, and could actually have some effect on an atmosphere—

The scene on the screen shifted. The vast mass of the cloud now appeared on the screen. It bulked to the right, galactic inclination, of Alondra. Now it was very close to the uninhabited outermost planet.

Then further, more worrying sensor readings started coming in. According to the *Enterprise's* detectors, the cloud was composed of gaseous matter so thick in some places that it bordered on the solid. It was too thick to be a nebula, too thin to be a world. It neither rotated nor tumbled, showing splendid disregard for all the usual effects of motion and solar gravitation. Pallas I and II should be having all kinds of effects on it now, yet sensors continued to claim the cloud ignored the twin suns completely.

And it moved rapidly. Much too rapidly.

There it was, then. The seemingly bottomless Pandora's box of the universe had confronted them with yet another surprise.

"Come, Mr. Spock. Keep at the computer. Let's have

further information," and, he didn't add, information that made a little more sense. Spock paused, looked up from his viewer.

"I'm sorry, Captain. I find myself quite intrigued by the phenomenon. There is both matter and energy active in the cloud, it seems. But to say the least, the combination is highly unorthodox. For example, the quantities of each do not appear to remain constant, but rather exist in a continual state of flux.

"This would imply that matter within the cloud is being steadily converted to energy. Yet it does not radiate more than a trickle of this apparent production."

"You're right, Spock, that's very intriguing." Kirk pondered. The closer they got, the more information they obtained, the more impossible this thing became. "It's very odd. It almost suggests . . ."

"Look!" Everyone whirled to face the screen at Sulu's abrupt shout.

The cloud had reached Alondra. Sulu switched hurriedly to long-range visual pickup and before their horrified eyes, the cloud slowly crept amoebalike across the face of the planet. It traveled over the planetary surface patiently, inexorably, and—one couldn't help but feel—deliberately.

Only Arex, mindful perhaps of Kirk's earlier reproof, kept his eyes on his instruments.

"Captain," he announced finally, "Alondra has disappeared from navigation scan." That sent Spock's gaze back to his library viewer.

Uhura suggested, "The cloud has come between us and the planet. Somehow that's interrupting scan."

"No, Lieutenant," said Spock quietly. "The cloud has engulfed Alondra." A long pause followed. The bridge was silent except for the tiny, nonconversational ticks and hums of various instruments. The next time he spoke, the science officer's voice conveyed an unmistakable feeling of alarm.

"Captain! The planet seems to be breaking up. Sensors indicate a definite and rapid reduction of planetary mass."

A hurricane of thoughts had roared through Kirk's

head in the past few minutes. Now he found himself voicing the least palatable of them.

"Spock," he asked quietly, "is it possible that this 'cloud' *consumes* planets?"

"Captain, I believe that your question is unnecessarily replete with emotional overtones."

"This whole situation is unnecessarily replete with emotional overtones, Mr. Spock. Please answer the question."

"Extrapolating from all available sensor information, sir," his first officer replied, argumenative to the last, "it would seem a reasonable assumption."

"Sir?" Kirk looked over at Sulu. "The cloud is changing course."

"Ridiculous, Mr. Sulu. It's not a powered vehicle. A natural object should not—"

"Course change verified, sir!" added Arex excitedly. "Initial course computation revision indicates—" he paused, triple-checking his figures, "indicates it is moving now in the direction of the second planet."

"But if it continues on that course—" Uhura called.

Kirk's voice was grim. "—Eighty-two million people will die."

Very quiet it was on the bridge then. Only the computers continued to converse.

"Mr. Sulu, prepare to increase speed to warp-eight. Push it to the limit. Inform Engineer Scott of the reasons, if he so inquires."

"Yes, sir," Sulu nodded. Kirk continued.

"At warp-eight, Mr. Sulu, we will intercept the cloud." At that Sulu looked back hesitantly towards the command chair, his gaze full of questions.

"We ... will ... intercept ... the ... cloud," Kirk repeated distinctly. He was well aware everyone on the bridge was staring at him. Well, what the hell did they expect? "And before it reaches the inhabited planet, Mantilles. Despite the fact that we are still uncertain as to the cloud's true nature. Despite the fact that it masses many millions of *Enterprise*'s.

"Ready, Mr. Sulu!"

"Course plotted and set, Captain."

"Warp-eight, please, Lieutenant."

Sulu did a small thing. Only God and helmsmen could warp the very fabric of space—and at times like these, some helmsmen got the two confused.

That's why navigation officers and chief engineers had the highest rate of turnover and mental crackup in Starfleet.

The *Enterprise* responded and leaped ahead.

"If we can't stop it, Jim, millions of people will die."

Kirk swiveled his chair. "Hello, Bones. I know. Perhaps more."

"True, Doctor," continued Spock. "If planetary annihilation is indeed a part of this thing's nature, it might seek out worlds as instinctively as any animal seeks out food. It may even consume stars as well as planets—though it seems woefully small in comparison to even a small star."

"Almost as small as we are in comparison to it?" Kirk mused. Spock, naturally, did not smile.

"Almost, Captain. Yet we know nothing of the cloud's limitations. If it has such selective ability, it could prove a threat to every world in our galaxy."

"Bones?" McCoy moved to stand close to Kirk. Everyone on the bridge could imagine, or thought they could, what was going on in the captain's mind right now. So they resolutely ignored the resultant conversation.

"Bones, I need an expert medical opinion on mass psychology."

"Then you've come to the wrong place, Jim." The jest fell flat. "Seriously, I can venture opinions, but not expert ones."

"You're the best I've got, Bones. Tell me—do we dare tell the people on Mantilles what we know? So that they can attempt to save at least a portion of the population? They have instruments, they can guess—but they won't know until it's too late."

McCoy looked up at the screen at the moving cloud. The distant view showed no bulging eyes, no gaping jaws. In appearance it was no more threatening than a cloud of steam.

"How much time do they have?"

Arex supplied the answer, and Kirk didn't even think

of reprimanding the lieutenant for evesdropping. "Four hours, ten minutes, sir."

McCoy looked at Kirk. "I suspect the people on Mantilles are organized, well-educated, civilized, thinking human beings, Jim."

Kirk nodded in confirmation. "That's how I see it, too, Bones. They'll panic, all right." McCoy grinned tightly.

"On the other hand, Captain," reminded Spock, and it was natural that he should be the one to voice the thought, "they may still manage to save some small portion of the populace."

"A great deal could depend on the executive in charge, Jim," McCoy continued. "Who's the governor of Mantilles? Do you know anything about him?"

"Robert Wesley," Kirk murmured, thinking back in time to a long-past incident. "He was in Starfleet once. Left it to accept the governorship." He glanced meaningfully up at the doctor. "He's no hysteric."

McCoy didn't hesitate. "Then tell him."

"Coming up on the cloud," interrupted Sulu. "ETA five minutes ten seconds."

"Very well, Lieutenant." Kirk whispered back at McCoy, "Thanks, Bones." Then he raised his voice and gave orders to Uhura.

"Lieutenant, send a priority one call to Governor Wesley on Mantilles."

"Aye aye, sir."

As the *Enterprise* gained distance on the cloud, viewscreen perspective had to be forced down once, twice—yet a third time. Then it was impossible to widen the view or reduce it any further.

There was nothing in the screen now but the shifting, enigmatic, threatening cloud-shape. It blotted out the universe.

Bland as the actual picture was, it exerted a tremendous fascination. Everyone stared at the nearing, gaseous form. Everyone but Spock. He found more of interest in his computer readouts.

"Captain, I'm getting anticipated readings from the chemical analysis sensors."

"Anticipated, Mr. Spock? Oh, you mean . . ."

"Yes, Captain. They are most unusual, in keeping with the unique nature of the cloud."

"Well, don't keep us in suspense any longer, Spock. What kind of readings?"

"There are indications of elements present in the cloud that are utterly unknown in our periodic tables, sir—both natural and artificial. I am now ninety percent certain of what has heretofore been only theory."

"Which is?" Kirk prompted.

"That this object has originated outside our galaxy."

"Captain!" yelled Sulu abruptly. They all turned back to face the screen.

A segment of the massive shape was twisting, bulging with ponderous speed. From the bulge long tendril-like spiral streamers of thick cloud suddenly reached out, out, in the direction of the *Enterprise*. Once formed, the fluffy pseudopods moved with uncanny speed and flexibility.

"Evasive action!" Kirk shouted, hands reflexively trying to dig into the metal of the command seat.

"Aye, sir!" shouted Arex as he and Sulu worked frantically at the helm.

But this close to target, evasive action was nearly impossible to coordinate. The *Enterprise* was no hummingbird, to spin on its own axis or suddenly fly backwards. Even if the fabric of the ship could have survived such a maneuver, everyone and everything on board would have been thrown out through the forward superstructure by sheer inertia.

It was like being attacked by a ball of loose cotton. The long streamers entwined themselves gently about the *Enterprise*. Then, warp-eight or no warp-eight, space-twisting engines or no space-twisting engines, the ship began to retract steadily back into the cloud.

"Full reverse thrust," ordered Kirk, more hopeful than sanguine.

"Full back engines, sir," Sulu confirmed. The bridge shuddered under the strain.

Except for computer-field compensation, the *Enterprise* would have been torn apart by the titanic conflicting stresses suddenly imposed on it. But the immense power of her engines was insufficient to pull her free.

"Not enough—it's not enough," McCoy said tightly, verbalizing the obvious.

"Some sort of antiplasma," Spock informed them, as if he were analyzing the composition of a candy bar. He looked up from the viewer. "It generates an unusually powerful attractive force. Not gravity as we know it, but similar." Kirk hardly heard him.

"Prepare to fire all phasers into the cloud mass. If possible, aim at where these tendrils connect with the mass itself."

"Locked on," said Sulu mere seconds later.

"Phasers ready," added Arex.

"Fire!"

"Firing phasers."

Ravening, destroying beams of pure force lanced out from the *Enterprise*—only to vanish with no visible effect into the cloud mass. They might as well have been beaming at the sun.

"Nothing, Captain," reported Sulu. Spock supplied an answer for the incredible.

"The cloud appears to have the ability to absorb energy, Captain. This is not surprising in view of what we already know about it. The beams of our phasers were not reflected by any sort of shield. Of course, anything that can manage the breakdown of a planet's molten core—"

There was no need to finish the thought. Try to harpoon a whale with toothpicks!

The streamers continued to pull the *Enterprise* closer to the cloud. Sulu was the first to notice the rippling in the surface of the roiling mass. A small opening appeared, expanded.

Its warp-drive engines still fighting in reverse, the starship disappeared into the cloud.

Kirk's stomach, on the other hand, was moving upwards and any minute now he was sure it would pop right out his mouth. The lights on the bridge fluttered, dimmed, and fluctuated wildly. Uhura was thrown out of her chair by an especially violent concussion.

Sulu was tossed a meter into the air before being

slammed down to the deck, while Kirk and Spock held onto their respective chairs for dear life.

Only Lt. Arex, with his three arms and legs, managed to retain anything like a stable position.

Fortunately, the severe shaking lasted only a few seconds. Buffeting became rapidly less and less violent. In a little while the ship had completely recovered its normal equilibrium.

"Uhura?"

She scrambled back into her seat, grimacing at the lingering pain, and started checking her console for breakage.

"Sore backside, Captain, that's all. Nothing vital damaged."

"That's a matter of opinion," McCoy disputed. Everyone was too tense for a really honest laugh, but the sortie took the edge off their initial shock. Kirk even managed to smile. As usual, Spock stared blankly at his chuckling comrades.

"Mr. Sulu?" Kirk called when the stifled laughter had stilled, "are you operational?" He tried to make a joke of it. The navigation officer was in obvious pain and just as obviously trying to hide it.

"I believe—there is a possibility my left leg is broken, Captain."

"Report to Sick Bay, Lieutenant." But Sulu showed no signs of leaving.

"If you don't mind, Captain," he replied, already checking his computer to establish their position, "I'd like to stay at the helm." Another flash of pain showed on his face, but he turned away from the others and Kirk had only a glimpse of it.

McCoy objected loudly, heading in Sulu's direction. "Lieutenant, I order you to—" Then he paused. Now more than ever Kirk was going to need the senior navigation officer's abilities. "All right, Mr. Sulu, you can remain at station as long as I can put that leg in a temporary splint."

McCoy set about his task.

Sulu watched his viewscreen, wincing only now and then.

"All right, Mr. Sulu," Kirk called. The viewscreen had gone blank. "See what you can get on the scanners." Sulu worked several controls.

Nothing happened.

"Emergency backup, Mr. Sulu." Immediately Sulu was manipulating an alternate set of switches. The screen started to clear, a picture to form—and there was a concerted gasp from the bridge.

The scene in the main screen was weird and beautiful. They appeared to be floating in a misty fog over a wavering, fantastic landscape of muted grey and brown. Huge, monolithic icebergs—shards of the planet Alondra—drifted with them in the mist. Many of the fragments were the size of large asteroids. They dwarfed the *Enterprise* whenever they moved close.

McCoy found further reason for amazement.

"We're still intact," he mused wonderingly, "but we must be inside the cloud!"

Uhura checked in. "All decks report considerable shaking up, Captain, but only slight damage." Sulu looked up from his station.

"Captain, objects approaching off the bow. Coordinates, well," he gestured at the viewscreen, "there they are."

A moment later a pair of huge, irregularly shaped blobs hove into view. Kirk didn't need sensor readings to tell him that they were heading towards the *Enterprise*. They were moving with impressive speed. Their size increased to threatening proportions as the distance between them and the trapped starship decreased.

"Deflector shields up and operating," informed Arex. He'd initiated deflector operation without Kirk's command—in this case, the sign of a good officer. There was a time and place for protocol—and a time and place to ignore it.

"More objects approaching aft!" added Sulu excitedly.

Kirk studied the clumsy, growing shapes intently. There was nothing to mark them as belligerent. They were utterly devoid of stinger, claw, fang, or for that matter, any other surface feature. It was the deliberateness of their approach, the indication of clear purpose in the way they moved towards the *Enterprise* that hinted at unfriendly intentions.

The cloud was also devoid of surface features.

"Analysis, Spock?"

"Nothing elusive or concealed about these, Captain," the science officer responded. "They are some organized form of highly charged antimatter."

At that point the highly charged voice of Chief Engineer Scott filtered over an intercom.

"Engineering to Captain Kirk." Kirk hit the broadcast switch on the arm of his chair.

"Kirk here. What's up, Scotty?"

"Captain," answered Scott ominously, "this drain on the deflector shields is too great for them to hold for any length of time."

"I know, Scotty." Kirk took another quick glance at the screen. Now the distinctive bright red of the blobs was pulsing visibly. As their color heightened in brilliance, one couldn't escape the impression that they were readying—something.

"Scotty, prepare the shields to deliver an antimatter charge. I can't tell you how strong it has to be, but you can be ready to give more than a tickle."

There was a brief pause, as though Scott was thinking about saying something. But only a firm, "Aye, Captain," came from the speaker.

Sulu shifted his eyes from the screen, kept them glued to the console until a rarely activated light winked on.

"Antimatter charge ready, sir." The gigantic blobs were almost on top of the ship.

"Discharge!" Sulu jammed in the switch.

Instantly, although there was no visible explosion, no blinding flare of light, the two amorphous masses fell back from the *Enterprise*. There was an isolated cheer from Uhura, but it died quickly. Their relief from the alien assault was only temporary.

A short distance away the blobs slowed, paused, and stopped. Everyone on the bridge waited breathlessly. Then they began to advance on the starship once again. But there were hopeful signs. The powerful antimatter charge the *Enterprise*'s engines had delivered had had some effect.

The bright crimson color of the two aggressive forms had faded, the sharp pulsing seemed weaker. Now both were a light shade of pink.

"Double the charge, Mr. Sulu."

"Sir?" Sulu looked doubtful. Kirk's reply was not.

"I said double the charge."

Sulu did things with the console. "Ready, sir."

Kirk watched, waited until the two monstrous shapes seemed ready to envelop the ship, then, "Discharge!"

The lobs hesitated, shuddered—and began to fall away from the *Enterprise*. As they did so their color shifted from pink to light pink, to white. Then the massive shapes started to break up, to dissolve into smaller and smaller pieces which then vanished into nothingness.

Nervous conversation filled the bridge. Everyone seemed to have something to say, except Spock. His mind was obviously elsewhere.

"Well, Spock, any conclusions?"

"Only the beginning of a theory, Captain. A hint of a hypothesis." He dropped the bombshell with maddening calm. "It is possible that this cloud in which we are entrapped is a living thing. A conscious, animate entity. It is my considered opinion, barring future data to the contrary, that it is alive."

Arex whistled. There were similar exclamations of surprise and shock from the others.

"That's a sweet one, Spock." Kirk's initial impulse was to reject the incredible statement out of hand. A living being eight hundred thousand kilometers across! Insane!

Yet Spock, while unshockable himself, would be fully cognizant of the effect such a pronouncement would have on the rest of them. He might call it a theory, he might call it mere hypothesis, but he wouldn't mention it unless he felt pretty damn sure of his supportive evidence. So Kirk swallowed his natural reactions and instead turned calmly to Bones. Such caution had saved him embarrassment more than once.

"How about you, Bones? Any opinions?" McCoy, he noticed, had been using the library-computer annex to run some questions of his own.

"There's certainly some resemblance, Jim. I don't know how much we can depend on that. But I can tell you one thing. We have to get out of this area. Those mists out there," and he nodded in the direction of the screen, which showed only a thin grey fog, "have, according to the latest readouts from our chemical sensors, many of the characteristics of macromorphase enzymes.

"If the shields should fail—and they won't stay up forever, not under this pressure—the hull will be rapidly corroded through and we'll all be broken down into nice, bite-sized, digestible particles."

"I am inclined to agree with the doctor, Captain," said Spock, staring into the computer viewer. "I have been running continual checks on the planet Alondra. Its ruptured mass has been steadily growing smaller ever since we entered the cloud. Energy levels, concurrently, are up. The obvious analogy is inescapable."

"It's converting mass into energy, of course," Kirk agreed, startled at how easily the stunning words came. "Even so, we—"

Everyone glanced up in alarm at a loud, raucous blast of sound. It came from Uhura's station. She recovered from her initial surprise, checked her station, and hastily lowered the volume.

"Captain. I have a subspace message from Governor Wesley on Mantilles." She paused, looked away in mild embarrassment. "I forgot. I was able to initiate the requested call to him before we were—pulled in."

Kirk considered. He could take the call right here, of course. But the fewer people who knew of the ultimate decisions taken with regard to the doomed world, the better. Word could always slip out somehow, and there might be personnel on board the *Enterprise* with relatives or close friends on the outpost planet. He had enough crises to handle.

He rose. "I'll take the call in my quarters, Lieutenant."

"Yes, sir."

"Mr. Sulu, Mr. Spock—utilize our scanners to assemble a chart of the cloud's composition and interior structure. Then give it to the library for analysis and preparation of initial diagrams. It's time we knew where we were." He turned and was on his way to his cabin before the two "yes, sirs" reached him.

# X

The short walk from the elevator to his quarters gave him a few precious seconds to think. The number of options open to him now was severely limited, and growing smaller by the minute. It didn't take much time to examine them all.

Eighty-two million souls.

*Poof.*

He shook his head and cursed the vilest curses he could think of. There were times when he wanted to take the old, antique projectile weapon out of its protective case in the officer's lounge and blast away at everything fragile and delicate in sight. That was the trouble with modern weapons. Phasers had no recoil, made no more noise than a door buzzer. Their destructive capabilites were considerable; their psychological value to the wielder, nil.

Eighty-two million. The death of ten or twenty intelligent beings at one time he could grasp, could comprehend. But this—it was too overwhelming, too enormous a figure to terrify. An entire world reduced to a loose mathematical abstraction.

Only the people who lived on it were real.

Bob Wesley was only slightly older than Kirk. His manner as he stared out from Kirk's private screen was calm, steady, competent. His face held a few more lines and his hair was greyer. The subtle assassins of politics could be harder on a man than all the terrors of space.

Now he looked even older than his years. He made no attempt to conceal the burden he was feeling, to hide the agony he felt. When the image first materialized on the tiny screen, Kirk was shocked. Kirk tersely gave Wesley the facts.

"Three and a half hours, Jim," said Wesley slowly, each word rolling and booming like the clang of a great bell. "It's not enough. Not nearly enough. Even if I had the ships available to really evacuate." Kirk tried to think of something encouraging to say, could only come up with honesty.

"You have time to save some *people,* Bob."

Wesley mumbled a reply. "If the word gets out—and it will, no matter how hard we try to keep it secret—it will only start the panic sooner." He coughed softly. "But you're right, of course. We must do what little we can."

Kirk had never seen a man look so helpless. He wondered how he'd be standing up to the pressure if their positions were reversed. Strong men had committed suicide out of inability to cope with far less crushing situations.

Self-destruction, at least, was not Bob Wesley's way.

"How—," Kirk found himself choking on the words, "how are you going to choose?" Wesley's answer was expected.

"There is no choice, Jim. We'll save some of the children." He made a tired gesture of dismissal.

"And now if you'll excuse me, Jim. I'd like to talk—it's been a long time—but I've many things to do. There's not much time left."

"Sure, Bob." Kirk strove to sound cheerful. It came out false. "I'll talk to you later, if there's anything new." Wesley shrugged slightly.

"If you want." He sounded like a dead man already. Composed and resigned to an inevitable fate. The screen abruptly went dark. Kirk stared at it for long minutes, thinking. Gradually his brows drew together, and his teeth ground against one another in silent anger.

By the time he'd reached the bridge again the cloud of

depression that had begun to overtake him, too, had been thrown aside by an invincible determination, a resolve to do *something*.

But *how?*

In three hours and twenty minutes the cloud would reach Mantilles. If that were permitted to happen millions of people would die. The elevator reached the bridge, and he stepped through the doors.

Very well—it must *not* be permitted to happen.

It was as simple as that.

He stopped, returned the stares of each and every one of the officers present. When he finally resumed his seat again and spoke, the words were directed at Spock and McCoy.

"Come on, gentlemen. I need your help. Your analyses, evaluations, opinions—no matter how wild, how outrageous. Exercise your minds, dammit! We're going to find a solution—and *no* one on Mantilles is going to die."

To an outsider familiar with the situation, it would have sounded futile. But somehow, at that point in time on the bridge, it didn't. In fact, it seemed almost reasonable.

"Start with basics," he finished. There was silence on the bridge.

"If we assume the cloud is a living being," said Spock slowly, "then it must follow that it requires some form of continual nourishment to sustain itself."

Kirk nodded. "And we have postulated that the cloud lives on the energy it converts from the mass of the planets it consumes—in this case, the planet Alondra. Though as yet we have no firm proof of this."

"Quite so," Spock added. "But it is apparently like some huge animal grazing here and there in the pasture of the universe."

That poetic phraseology caused Doctor McCoy to miss twelve full lines of computer biological analysis. He had to back up the tape and rerun the information.

"All right," agreed Kirk, hand caressing chin. "Let's follow that line of thought through. Bones, what about those antagonistic blobs?"

"Offhand, judging from the way they reacted to our

presence, I'd say they perform essentially the same function as teeth, Jim. They break up the largest chunks of matter for easier digestion. Maybe they sensed us as being larger than we were, because compared to those chunks of planet floating around in here, we're digestible-size already. Possibly our engines give off enough energy to fool them into thinking we're more nutritious than we really are."

Kirk nodded, turned to face Sulu.

"Lieutenant, the computer scanners should have come up with something on the cloud's internal composition and makeup by now. Let's see it."

"Yes, sir." Sulu turned to his console. "Computer schematic readied. Coming on."

He hit a switch. On the screen, for the first time, they had an overall view of the interior of their massive host.

In shape it was rather like a fat pair of disembodied human lungs, joined directly together. Instead of a trachea or esophagus there was a bottle-shaped bulge in its middle. Rising from the top of this pear-shape was another long, narrower cavity.

From the top of this area a long cylindrical passage appeared to open into space at the top of the cloud.

Thus reduced to screen-size and roughly drawn, the diagram looked insignificant, almost comical, like a child's drawing. But after what had happened to Alondra, no one felt inclined to laugh.

The problem was that the chart put the alien into too-easy perspective. The tiny white dot representing the *Enterprise,* for example, could not be shown to scale. It was much too big. In reality the cloud was too big to comprehend. As a diagram, it was reduced wrongly to a harmless crude shape.

Still, there were things to be learned from it, and Kirk studied the drawing intently. For him, at least, the drawing induced no false sense of security.

The outlines of the cloud's interior were not fixed, but appeared to flow and change as befitted a mostly gaseous organism. Anyhow, it was still solid enough for him to comment, "It seems to have some kind of regularized anatomy. That opening where we were first pulled in doesn't show. It must have closed fast right behind us.

"But there looks to be some kind of permanent opening up near the top."

"I don't know, Jim," chipped in McCoy, immediately picking up the captain's line of thought. "If this thing also has some kind of colossal digestive system ahead of us, I don't see how we could make it that far."

"Three hours, five minutes, sir," announced Arex dispassionately, "till the cloud reaches Mantilles." Kirk nodded acknowledgment of this information. He'd already made his decision. If nothing else, time dictated a move at this stage.

"Since we appear to have only one way out, we must try it. Mr. Sulu, take us to that central core area."

"Aye, aye, sir." Kirk put his right elbow on the arm of the control chair and rested his chin in the waiting palm. A slight smile parted his lips.

"And if this thing *does* have a stomach, we just might be able to give it a bad enough case of indigestion to make it turn from Mantilles—"

It didn't take long for them to reach the edge of the area the computer had pinpointed as the cloud's central cavity. There was only one bar to further progress.

The entrance to that cavity was closed.

Closed by a pulsing, vaguely irislike valve.

"We've reached the entrance to the central core, Captain," confirmed Sulu. McCoy laughed nervously as he studied their intended path.

"What do we do now—knock?"

The ship gave a sudden lurch. But this one was bearable and no one was hurt. It was nowhere near as violent as the severe jolts that had pounded them when they were first drawn into the cloud mass.

"No need, Bones," murmured Kirk tightly. "Here we go . . ."

The iris was opening.

Swept like a leaf on a tidal bore, the *Enterprise* was tossed into the core area, along with floating mist and several still gigantic chunks of the planet Alondra. Then the iris closed ponderously behind them.

The scene in the central core was as radically different from the areas they'd already passed through as it was from the naked blackness of space itself. This core section was a kaleidoscope of colors, a flaring, scintillating, rainbowed chamber spotted with constant awesome explosions.

Huge slender pyramid shapes protruded from the side of the core wall they were drifting near. As they stared at the screen, a large section of planet drifted close by one, seemed to hesitate in space, touched—

A detonation that would have shamed anything smaller than a sunspot filled the viewscreen with blinding, pure white light. The glare faded rapidly. If the scanners hadn't automatically darkened to compensate for the shocking flash their eyes could have been seriously damaged. As it was, they were only impressed.

When they could see clearly again the first thing everyone noted was that the section of Alondra had disappeared. But the slender pyramid it had impacted on was glowing incandescent with residual energy—energy produced by their meeting and the resultant explosion.

A shock wave struck the *Enterprise* soon after, but the first flash had given the ship's computers necessary seconds to brace for the powerful side effects. After all, they were still operating at planetary distances from the wall. The ship wasn't damaged.

Explosions continued to occur at regular intervals, some weaker, some more powerful than the first. While the *Enterprise* rode the resultant shock waves easily, the constant rocking and buffeting hampered observation and made accurate navigation increasingly difficult.

Still, the starship managed to pick a path through the central core. By keeping it in one piece and on course, a sweating Sulu and Arex were earning their rank.

Uhura watched the pyramid destruction/growth cycle wonderingly. "What *are* those things?"

McCoy had been making analogies as well as observations. "I'm going to make an educated guess." He took a deep breath, let it out slowly. "I think we're now moving in what corresponds in man to the small intestine. Those shapes growing out of the core wall seem to be somewhat similar in basic function to human villi."

"Villi?" Kirk looked back questioningly at the doctor. Physiology, human or otherwise, had never been one of his favorite subjects. It seemed he'd spent too much time on spatial physics, astrodynamics, and administrative operations. True, a starship captain is supposed to have at instant beck and call only slightly less information than a ship's computer banks, but even so . . .

McCoy nodded. "The human small intestine is lined with millions of them, although they are more or less permanent. They don't destroy themselves on contact with food, as these seem to. They absorb nutrients into the body by—"

As McCoy droned on with his biological comparisons, everyone on the bridge had plenty of time to study the actual process. Though it was hard to compare the titanic forces at work on the screen to what was taking place beneath one's own stomach.

A section of some great mountain was drawn to a villus and, following the now familiar pattern, disintegrated brilliantly on contact. The villus grew alarmingly as it absorbed the energy generated by the explosion.

At the same time the long pyramid shape disappeared. Or more accurately, shrank back into the core wall. Immediately, a new pyramid began to form and stretch outward slightly to the left of where the first had vanished.

That's when Spock looked up excitedly from his position at the library.

"Captain, according to conclusive sensor readings, those villi-analogs are composed of solid antimatter! If the *Enterprise* should touch one . . ."

". . . we'll disappear faster than a piece of chocolate in a phaser beam," Kirk finished. "Mr. Sulu, keep those shields up at all costs!"

"I'll try, sir."

Kirk returned his attention to the screen. The *Enterprise* continued to drift through the chaotic core. In some ways, the continuous mass-energy conversion cycle reminded him of a thermonuclear reaction—slowed down many times.

"Incredible, simply incredible," he whispered. "So much power—" He watched another chunk of world vanish in a shattering display of energy. There was enough power being produced here to drive endless fleets of starships, to light entire inhabited worlds. All wasted.

However, he reminded himself, the creature would consider it otherwise. If it was capable of considering anything, which he sincerely doubted.

"The villi reabsorb with the energy they take in and immediately begin to regenerate preparatory to repeating the cycle." Spock agreed.

"It is clearly all part of the natural digestive process in operation here, Captain. Sensors indicated when we first entered that a natural force-field of vast dimensions was in operation in this core area. At first I was unsure as to its purpose. Now it is perfectly clear. The field serves to contain the matter-antimatter contact/dissolution sequence and keep it within manageable bounds.

"Otherwise the creature would quite literally eat itself to death."

A telltale on Uhura's main board winked for attention, was instantly shunted to the main speaker.

"Engineering to bridge." Kirk hit the reply switch.

"Yes, Scotty?"

"Keepin' the deflectors this high is putting an enormous strain on the engines, Captain. Especially on our antimatter power supply. What with the continual maximum *power* demands on the shields as well, our reserve energy supplies are fallin' fast. Too fast."

Too fast, too fast—! Everything was happening too fast. Damn a universe which had infinity at its command and yet no time to spare!

"How much time have we got left, Scotty?"

"Twenty-one minutes, Captain—and there's no safety margin figured into that. That's *everything*. But if the power indicator drops below two antikilos, we'll not have even that. The engines won't have enough antimass to sustain reaction. We'll lose motive power as well as shields and deflectors."

"Thank you, Mr. Scott. I'll keep that information in mind." He snapped off the intercom and looked to the helm. "Push our speed, Mr. Arex. I know it isn't easy to maneuver in here, but we must make our way through the opening at the other end of this core."

Arex's voice was tight in reply. "Yes, sir. We'll make it, sir."

Long minutes passed while the *Enterprise* picked its way at high speed through the weird jungle of gigantic villi, surrounded by unceasing detonations of unimaginable power.

For a while it seemed they'd make the core exit with no trouble. Then—perhaps Arex or Sulu miscalculated slightly, or maybe their speed was simply too great for a particularly tight passage.

Spatial gyros screamed in sudden protest as computer emergency overrides strove to correct position. They were drifting towards one of the waiting villi.

"I can't hold it on course, sir!" Sulu yelled desperately. "I'm using full power!"

"Increase deflector screens to maximum."

"Deflector screens to maximum," Arex acknowledged.

The starship shuddered, straining to pull away. One of the huge slender pyramids seemed to leap out at them, reaching hungrily and growing gigantic in the viewscreen. Enormous—

It stayed enormous, but abruptly was growing no larger. And then it began to move, to shift out of view as the *Enterprise* shuttled pass.

Kirk tried to relax a little and found he couldn't. His muscles were knotted tighter than a reaction coil. Another pass that close to one of the villi and the deflector shields would surely collapse under the immense load. Once that happened, so would every atom that comprised the *Enterprise* and her crew.

The speaker cleared again. Another call from Scott. Kirk was half expecting it. That last narrow escape had used up any safety margin they might have had.

The question now was, did they have any margin at all?

"Take over, Mr. Spock," he said when Scotty had finished detailing their present status. "I'm going down to Engineering."

"Very well, Captain."

Scott was waiting for him when the elevator opened onto the main engineering deck. The chief said nothing, but went instead to a nearby console and indicated an especially eloquent gauge. The instrument said everything for him. It showed the level of reserve power currently available in the central antimatter reaction chambers.

Showed it hovering uncertainly right around the two-kilo mark.

"There it is, Captain. All the wishin' in the world won't change that level. If we don't stop the excessive power drain right now, it'll be the end of us."

"It'll be the end of us if we do, Scotty. You're a master engineer—in many ways this is more your ship than it is mine. Think of something!"

"Well," Scott's expression showed that he'd been pondering an idea for some time but even now was reluctant to voice it.

"Come on, Scotty—if it's anything more concrete than prayer, I'm willing to listen to it." He'd already tried the former, to no avail.

"Captain, all our sensor reports indicate that those 'villi' pyramid converters are antimatter—antimatter of high energy potential, to say the least.

"If we could somehow obtain a bit of it—an infinitesimal amount to the creature—it might serve just as well as normal antimatter fuels. Put it in the engine, and unless it has utterly unique physical properties, it ought to regenerate reaction. We'd have enough power to drive the ship at maximum and hold both shields and deflectors at same."

Kirk looked thoughtful. "That would take care of our lack of antimatter, sure. But we also need matter engines regenerated."

Scott smiled. "Matter's no problem, sir. I've already had my people working on beaming aboard some of the loose planet floatin' free around us. There's enough matter here to power a million starships.

"As for the antimatter, we can't touch it—or let it

touch anything solid, of course. I've considered the difficulties fully, Captain. It's not like cuttin' firewood. But I think there's a good chance we could cut it with a neutral tractor beam and then transport it aboard."

"Transport it aboard?" Kirk looked uncertain. "If it contacts the inside of the ship or any of us, for even a microsecond, it'll be the finish just as surely as if we'd rammed one of the villi."

"That won't happen, Captain," Scott objected eagerly. "I'm sure I can rig a force-field box that will hold the antimatter suspended in its center. A smaller, cruder version of the machinery normal fueling stations use. Then I can shift the whole thing by portable tractor beam into the antimatter nacelle. The small generator and controls for the field itself can be disintegrated the second the engines start to regenerate.

"Once we manage the initial transportin', the rest should be a simple matter." He noticed the odd expression on Kirk's face. "Sorry, sir, no pun intended."

"Don't give it a thought, Scotty—it doesn't matter." They smiled together. Then Kirk gave the chief engineer's proposal some serious consideration.

"Mr. Scott, this idea qualifies you for incarceration as a mental case. You realize that, don't you?"

"Yes, sir!"

"You've been under tremendous pressure lately and it's affected your thinking. Obviously you've been operating with several circuits loose."

"Yes, sir. Thank you, sir."

"Let's try the goddamn thing—"

Seconds later Scott was at the main engineering console, communicating his needs forward to Sulu. Then the two men headed for the transporter room on the run.

The *Enterprise* began to leave its weaving, bobbing course. It shifted as near as it dared to one villi. This protrusion had been selected because it was a little more isolated from its neighbors than most.

As Arex positioned them carefully, a tractor beam—its normal radiance lost in the glare of nearby eruptions—darted out from the ship and neatly excised a two-meter square chunk of the villi.

If the cloud-being felt this minute biopsy, it gave no sign.

"Got it, sir," announced Scott. Kirk was standing next to him in the main transporter room. "Mr. Kyle," Scott said to the transporter chief, "bring 'er aboard."

Kyle nodded. A large, dull metal cube with handles set into two sides rested on one of the transporter disks. Another side of the cube was filled with dials, switches, naked components and generating equipment. These produced and regulated the invisible force-field inside. The field-cube was not impressive, but it would hold with stability enough antimatter to destroy a fair-sized continent.

A familiar little multicolored glow appeared just above the upper rim of the box. Kyle made a hurried adjustment of the controls. The glow vanished.

Slowly, he brought down the single transporter lever in operation and let out a relieved sigh as it hit bottom.

"Sorry, sir," he said to Kirk. "Close. Almost materialized it outside the field."

"Good thing you didn't," Kirk agreed calmly. Meanwhile his insides were still jumping. All the antimatter had to do was contact the *air* in the room. That would have been enough to set it off.

"I presume it *is* inside now?" Kyle felt secure enough to nod even without checking his instrumentation.

Kirk, Scott, and a pair of technicians moved forward towards the placid yet threatening box. Scott held a small control device in one hand. They mounted the transporter platform and one by one, took a look into the open cube.

Inside, floating easily in vacuum, was the loose piece of villus.

"So that's what antimatter looks like," whispered Kyle uneasily. Like most of the *Enterprise's* personnel, his job never brought him in contact with the incredibly dangerous stuff. He could have done without this novelty, too.

"Doesn't look real, does it?" murmured Kirk. "It belongs more properly to the imagination. This material used to be the unicorn of atomic physics." He glanced abruptly at his chief engineer and his tone turned urgent. "Scotty, we've got ten minutes left."

Scott was checking the small instrument he held.

"Just wanted to make sure there was no oscillation in field strength, Captain. It's holding fine. Let's go."

He clipped the tiny rectangle to his belt. Then he and Kirk moved to stand on opposite sides of the cube. They gripped the handles and lifted. A tractor beam would have been easier, but riskier, too. Scott didn't want to use one field to move another. Funny things could happen sometimes when energy fields of different properties and function intersected.

Theoretically, the cube was full of nothing. There should be only the weight of the force-field box itself. But dammit, it *seemed* heavier!

Dropping it would have no effect on the field inside, of course. Nevertheless, they walked very, very carefully. Certain sections of the human mind were sometimes reluctant to believe what another part might tell it.

When the elevator doors dilated and they stepped into the main engineering room again, it seemed like the whole technical section was waiting for them. No one offered greeting. No one made idle conversation. They knew what was in the cube.

Still moving cautiously, Kirk and Scott angled towards the door marked:

ACCESS ROUTE–ANTIMATTER CONTROL

And underneath!

ABSOLUTELY AUTHORIZED PERSONNEL ONLY—*Starfleet Reg.E-11634.*"

One of the engineers operated the automatic safety door, and they entered the small service lift thus revealed. Neither man said anything as the lift carried them down and forward. It was a short ride. The door slid back.

They were in the antimatter nacelle.

A narrow walkway led down the middle of the chamber. Like the lift exit it glowed faintly with its own unceasing, permanent force-field.

If everything else on the *Enterprise* was to shut down, all power including life-support systems to fade—phasers, lights, engines—the small prelocked power supply that maintained this most vital function of the starship would remain activated and functioning.

If the entire crew were killed and every instrument on board destroyed, the starship would still be salvageable.

The field was necessary because nearly everything in the huge, cavernlike chamber except the lift exit and walkway—and themselves, of course—was composed of antimatter. This was the greatest accomplishment of Federation technology—engineering in negativity. The maintenance walkway they were on was suspended from walls, floor, and ceiling by force-field insulators.

Cell-like bins lined the walls like the inside of some enormous insectoid hive. Each had simple red, yellow, and green indicator lights on the outside. Everything in here was simple and functional. Antimatter was difficult to work with, and there was no room for extraneous detail. It would have been too dangerous.

Red lights gleamed on all of the bins—except for the one closest to the lift-exit door. As they passed it, this single remaining green light faded out. At the same time, the middle indicator began to glow a bright yellow.

Scott glanced quickly at it and then ahead down the walkway.

"Well, that gives us two minutes." They moved as fast as they could, almost running now. They had to be careful. Normally the force-fields surrounding the walkway formed impenetrable barriers even a ground-car couldn't break through.

But now, as the main engines of the *Enterprise* began to die, the separate power supply that maintained the protective fields started to shift over to salvage mode. That meant using only enough power to keep the matter of the walkway, say, from contacting the antimatter of the chamber.

If they slipped and fell, they'd never feel the final impact, never know the moment of death. Because touching the floor here would mean destroying the instrument of touch, the attached you, and the entire ship.

It was a place for people with the patience and manipulative skill of surgeons. That's why the personality profile requirements for antimatter engineers were among the highest in the Federation.

At the far end of the walkway, which had seemed kilometers away, was a huge, unspectacular-looking circular chamber. Tubes radiated from it in all directions. An insulated instrument panel was set into the walkway nearby. Scott used his free hand to trip the comm switch.

"All right, Davis, we're here. Open it."

The single door of the chamber slid back with agonizing slowness. They carefully put the box inside the inner antimatter acceptance alcove. The door slid back automatically. There was a pause while the field cube was transferred to the inside of the main chamber.

Spock and Kirk hadn't waited to check on the automatic process. They'd dashed back to the lift door. Once there, Scott took the small control device from his belt. There was no time for a precheck, no time to see if the automatic partitioning device would dissolve the matter of the field cube in time.

A thumb descended at the same time as the yellow light on the nearby bin faded out.

A loud crackling noise like a ton of tin foil being crushed came from the area of the main chamber. There was a breathless pause. Then, a gentle violet hue appeared around it, seeming to issue from the chamber wall. Another crackling, softer, and suddenly the myriad webbing of tubes and lines extending from the central sphere also shone with violet radiance.

The luminescence reached to the bins. Rapidly, the indicator lights began to change—from red, to yellow, to bright emerald green, winking on in a reassuring fugue of color.

Even more reassuring was the steady hum of energy that had been nearly absent when they'd entered. Now it filled the antimatter nacelle.

"Scotty," breathed Kirk slowly, too exhausted to feel satisfied, "you've just given the *Enterprise* and Mantilles a chance to live."

Scott looked totally drained. "Thank you, sir. I don't think I want to go through this sort of thing very often. I'd much rather do it in theory."

# XI

Kirk was feeling rather optimistic—unreasonably so—when he resumed his position on the bridge. They had coped with a seemingly impossible power situation; they could cope with anything else. He spoke to his left.

"Situation update, Mr. Spock?" Spock looked up from the computer again. As usual, the recent emergency had had no visible effect on him. His expression was neither elated nor discouraging—only neutral.

"The cloud is now only forty-two minutes, fourteen seconds from Mantilles, Captain. And while you were with Mr. Scott in the antimatter nacelle, I was able to ascertain an important fact. I might venture to say, even, a vital fact." His eyebrows went up, and as usual Kirk's attention intensified at that inadvertent signal. Something significant was up.

"This creature does have a brain."

If the creature had a brain, that implied the chance that—no, no—it was too much to hope for. Mad, in fact.

But then, this whole situation was mad.

Why mightn't it be consistently mad?

"Could . . . it possibly be intelligent, Spock?"

"It is far too early to guess, Captain. We really have no basis for such a supposition. Our information thus far is of purely anatomical nature. It has made only one action which might conceivably be interpreted as intelligent. It changed course from Alondra to move towards Mantilles."

Kirk shook his head frustratedly. "Not enough. We

can't go by that. It might just have been an involuntary response to a new source of food." What now?

"Let's see what the computer cartographic sensors have put together, Mr. Spock."

The first officer adjusted controls. A diagram of the cloud's interior appeared again on the screen. It was much enhanced since the last time he'd seen it. Considerable information had come in since then.

"A great deal of electrical activity emanates from that big, irregular-shaped object at the top of the core, Captain. Dr. McCoy has been studying that activity and I believe he has something to add."

"That's right, Jim. The impulses fall in regular patterns to an extent that would seem to preclude random generation. They might be normal for where this thing comes from, but . . . I'm inclined to regard those patterns as similar to those I've seen before."

"Before? Where, Bones?"

"Everywhere—whenever I take a cranial check on any crew member. They sure *look* like intelligent brain waves."

"It's so big," Kirk muttered. "Hellishly big." He paused thoughtfully. "But if we can reach it before the creature reaches Mantilles, we might be able to save the planet. Whether it's intelligent or not."

"Jim? I'm not sure I follow you."

"I'm not surprised, Bones. You're a physician. Your mind, your thoughts, your instincts are geared towards preserving life. You wouldn't think of using photon torpedoes to destroy a living mind."

"Captain," interrupted Spock, "this is as you say, a living creature. I am compelled to mention that Starfleet regulations—" But Kirk had no time to listen to a lecture on regulated morality.

"Sometimes, Mr. Spock, through no conscious fault of your own, your recourse to logic in every matter makes you sound something of an idiot. I am aware of the regulations regarding the killing of intelligent life-forms.

"But as you yourself admit, we don't know that this life-form is intelligent. When I have to balance that remote possibility against the lives of eighty-two million Mantillians—well, how long would you hesitate?"

"Of course, you are correct, Captain," replied Spock quickly. In moments like these he was reminded that he was a Vulcan speaking to humans. In such emotional moments it was often better to say nothing to them than to be logical. "I did not mean to imply that—"

"I know, I know, Spock," admitted Kirk tiredly. "You really had no control over what you said."

"Are you implying, Captain, that my reaction was emotional?" Even tempered or not, Spock managed to sound outraged. Tense moment or not, there were some things that couldn't be permitted to go unquestioned.

"No, no, no, Spock! You could only say the first logical thing that—this being being—oh hell, let's drop it."

"A most logical decision, Captain."

Kirk started to retort, then remembered that Spock had no emotional need to resort to sarcasm. Faced with disaster after disaster he was beginning to retreat into inanities. That was no way to inspire the confidence of his crew.

Kirk stared resolutely at the screen—and thought.

Eventually they reached the borders of the area the computer had labeled a brain. The new sector turned out to be made up of deep yellow cloud crisscrossed with pulsing white cables and lines that vanished in all directions. Spock and Uhura were using the sensors to prepare a detailed chart of the brain interior so that the *Enterprise*'s powerful torpedoes might be used to best advantage.

Scott was still keeping a close watch on his precious engines, so Uhura was handling the basic programming. McCoy remained on the bridge. He always felt—though Spock would have considered it absurd—completely useless in such moments.

At the same time McCoy hoped fervently his talents wouldn't be required. This constant paradox in tight situations was rough on even a well-balanced individual. That was one reason he made so many jokes. Laughter's therapeutic value was vastly underrated. But he wandered aimlessly about the bridge, trying to stay out of everyone's way and for the most part, succeeding.

In fact, this kept him free for one of his primary functions.

"Am I doing the right thing, Bones?" Kirk asked him quietly. "Starfleet prime directive number two prohibits the taking of intelligent life. I once said myself that man would not rise above primitiveness until he stood up and vowed, 'I will not kill today.'"

"You also said you couldn't let this thing wipe out over eighty million lives," McCoy countered gently. "Certainly that takes precedence over the second directive."

"I know, I know! Viewed objectively, or logically, as Spock would prefer—there is no choice. But I'm the one who has to live with the decision to kill."

Spock spared him further introspection. "Captain, I've completed the analysis of the target area. I am afraid your initial estimation of the destructive capability of the ship's photon torpedoes was badly overrated. According to my calculations, our entire offensive armament is insufficient to insure the creature's destruction, let alone incapacitation." He paused.

"However, there *is* one other possibility. The brain could be completely destroyed if we aimed the *Enterprise* at its center and then converted the entire ship to energy. Such a single overwhelming strike should prove mortal. It would certainly cripple the creature and remove its ability to hunt out specific worlds."

"That sounds like you're telling us to blow up the ship," guessed McCoy incredulously.

"I believe that is what I just said, Doctor." McCoy had no argument to counter with. Like the rest of them he'd been caught completely unprepared for the science officer's words.

Only Kirk wasn't shocked.

"I expect those figures on the limits of our photon torpedoes are accurate, Mr. Spock?" he queried. "You've checked and rechecked them, no doubt."

"Naturally," Spock replied. "I do not profess to be enamored of the idea of destroying ourselves, Captain. I have no more wish for self-destruction than anyone else. I merely report the facts as they exist and suggest alternative lines of operation for your consideration."

"But that is your recommendation?"

Spock nodded. "We seem to be left with no other alternative."

"Thank you, Mr. Spock." Kirk drummed fingers on the arm of the command chair. Spock was right. They'd run out of options—and were rapidly running out of time.

Even so, he hedged.

"You're sure it would do the job?"

"Yes, Cptain. Quite sure."

Kirk leaned over and spoke into the communicator grid. "Kirk to engineering."

"Engineering," came the distant voice. "Scott here."

Kirk composed himself and rehearsed the words in his mind. He wanted Scott to get it right the first time.

He remembered the last time he'd uttered the words, when they'd battled the strange energy-being in orbit around the bulk of a dead star. But in his mind he'd known that was a feint. A desperate one, but still a feint. A trick to frighten their unwanted passenger away. It had worked.

This time, however, it was different. He had no tricks in his mind, no hidden surprises to spring on this lumbering, alien entity. It was to be a kamikaze strike, plain and simple.

Idly, he wondered where that strange-sounding word had come from.

"Mr. Scott, prepare the self-destruct mechanism in the engines. Computer control for triggering the device will be here, on the bridge. Rig it with Lt. Uhura." There was a long pause at the other end. "Mr. Scott?"

"Aye, sir." Kirk clicked off and sat back. The following comment turned the atmosphere in the room topsy-turvy. It was typical of McCoy.

"Well, gentlemen, that's one decision you won't have to live with." Even Kirk smiled.

"Wait til you hear the next one, Bones. It'll kill you."

"What on Vulcan is the matter with you two?" queried Spock blankly.

"Nothing, Spock," McCoy was quick to counter. "You're right, as usual. As a comedy act, we're dying."

Kirk chuckled. "Stop it, Bones. That's an order." He paused, grinned even wider. "You're killing me."

Spock shook his head wonderingly. "Humans!" There was no contempt in the friendly exclamation. A little pity, perhaps.

Kirk's smile faded. They didn't need pity right now. They needed miracles.

Meanwhile, Uhura had nearly finished programming the cerebral diagram. A light flashed on her console as she was setting the schematic for display. She checked it, then swiveled around in her chair to look over at Kirk.

"Incoming communication, sir. It's Governor Wesley on Mantilles."

Kirk considered retreating to his cabin again to take the call, immediately squelched the idea. By the time the information reached the rest of the crew, the fate of the *Enterprise* and the eighty-two millions on Mantilles would already have been decided.

"Put it on the viewscreen here, Lieutenant."

"Yes, sir." She made the necessary connections. "Go ahead, Governor." Wesley's image strengthened on the screen.

Very little time had passed since his last conversation with Kirk, but he seemed to have aged years, not hours.

"Hello, Jim."

"Bob, is the evacuation proceeding?" Wesley nodded wearily. His words were delivered in a flat, even tone, interspersed with long sighs. The fresh attitude of determination that had gripped the *Enterprise* had no such counterpart on Mantilles.

"Yes, its started. We're doing as well as we can. Oh, there was some hysteria at the beginning. But the government's been very candid with them and they appreciate that. They've taken it well, all things considered. Damn well. Much better than we had any right to expect.

"I think the announcement that we're going to take only children made the potentially dangerous ones sit down and do some serious thinking. The few real nuts we were ready for." His face was a study in frustration.

"But it's only five thousand, Jim. Five thousand, out of

"I know," Kirk murmured compassionately. It sounded woefully inadequate, even presumptuous—but Christ, what else could he say?

Wesley's frustration found release in a burst of anger. "The hell you do! You sit up there safe in your starship and—" He caught himself right away. The anger vanished as quickly as it had come and he slumped in his seat. "I'm sorry, Jim. I'm ... sorry." Kirk said nothing this time. It was amazing that Wesley had managed to hang onto his sanity.

"We can see the cloud approaching, Jim. We have no more ships left."

Sulu's voice intruded, charonlike. "Thirty-one minutes, four seconds to Mantilles, sir." Kirk nodded absently.

"Bob, where's Katie?"

"Here." Wesley smiled and looked off-screen to his right. "With me."

That, somehow, settled things. He'd been ninety percent sure. Now it was complete.

"Don't worry, Bob. She'll be all right. I promise you that." He paused, tried to think of something else to say. There were many things, going all the way back to their days at Starfleet together. And no time. No time for any of them No time for anything more than a—

"Goodbye, Bob."

"Goodbye, Jim." The image faded from the screen. After a pause, McCoy spoke up.

"Who's Katie?"

"Hmmm?" Kirk had been deep in thought. Should he have told Wesley what they were going to try? No ... best not to raise false hopes. The Mantillians, it seemed, were resigned to their probable fate.

McCoy was waiting patiently. "Oh, sorry Bones. His daughter. She's eleven, I think. Spock, you commented on the vast area of this brain. Is there anyway at all we could contact a mind so huge, any way at all we could determine if it's intelligent? Perhaps a Vulcan mind touch—?"

"I had not considered it, Captain," replied the science officer, genuinely surprised. "I expect I was too close to the idea. But it would require physical contact. That is quite impossible." He paused, thinking.

"However, I might be able to reach out with my mind. There is an enormous quantity of electrical energy playing about the ship—the creature's thoughts. If we focus our sensor pickups on them, the resultant information could be routed through the library's phonetics/languages section for breakdown into comprehensible abstract idea structures—words. There is the strong possibility that none of these impulses represent anything as developed as reasoning thought . . ."

"But it's damn well worth a try," agreed Kirk. "Question is, can we handle it?"

"I can link in the universal translator," added Uhura excitedly, "and route the results through the audio systems from here!"

"Too many complicated linkups," Kirk complained. "But that's all mechanical. What really worries me is . . . can you do it in time?"

Spock considered. "It is impossible to calculate all the variables, Captain. There are a great many unknown factors. I make no promises."

Kirk noticed that he didn't mention another possibility . . . that contact with such an enormous mind might fatally overload his own.

Sulu, "Twenty-six minutes exactly to Mantilles, sir." Now who was wasting time?

"All right, Spock. Get on it." Spock and Uhura's stations became a center of feverish activity as technicians poured onto the bridge to help modify existing circuits and systems for a task their designers never dreamed of.

Kirk took a moment to take care of one other detail.

"Captain's log, star date 5372.1. This may very well be the last entry in the log of the U.S.S. *Enterprise*.

"It is only a matter of minutes before the cosmic cloud referred to in previous entry reaches Mantilles." He glanced back at Uhura's communications alcove. As his or her respective task was completed, the technicians began to leave the bridge. There were quiet murmurs of encouragement for Uhura and the rest of the regular bridge complement—especially for Spock.

"Science officer Spock has been working on the problems involved in reaching the cloud's thoughts—if it has any. But even should he succeed, I doubt there is enough time left for any meaningful exchange to take place. The possibility that we could persuade it to avoid Mantilles is . . ." He stopped.

If Uhura and Spock failed, no one would ever read this entry. It would vanish with the rest of the *Enterprise* and her crew in a matter-destroying holocaust of stellar magnitude.

If such a possibility appeared imminent while they were in free space, he could have shot the log clear. It was permanently mounted in a special, super-fast courier torpedo equipped with a powerful homing beacon. The entire setup was supposed to insure that even if a starship was visited with total destruction, it log—and perhaps the reasons for its destruction—would survive.

Its builders had not envisioned this particular situation, however. Once free of the *Enterprise*'s sustained shields and deflectors, the torpedo would be barely a snack for the cloud's energy-converting villi and amorphous drifting "teeth."

No, he would finish *this* entry only if Spock and Uhura were successful. The entry would conclude on a positive note, or not at all.

Located on the helm-navigation console between Sulu and Arex was a large digital chronometer. Efficient and obedient, it shifted a seven out of sight and replaced it with a six. It took no notice of its impending annihilation.

Kirk spared only a brief glance at the elevator when the last of the technicians filed out and Engineer Scott arrived. He'd have to handle the engineering from on-bridge station now. Uhura would be completely occupied with monitoring the complicated communications linkup system.

"Engineering reports all tie-ins completed and operating, sir. The procedure is ready."

"Thank you, Scotty." He looked at Spock and waited.

Spock made two final connections, checked an audio lead, and then moved to the library-computer station.

"Ready, Captain." Kirk and McCoy exchanged looks . . . perhaps their last, though neither man regarded it as such.

"You may proceed, Mr. Spock," Kirk whispered, not knowing why he did.

Spock turned in his chair and swiveled it towards the main viewscreen. He leaned back, closed his eyes, and extended both arms, hands and fingers together, straight out in front of his chest.

Several seconds passed. They seemed like days. Then his wrists began to turn slowly from side to side, rotating with near mechanical precision. Kirk had seen this before, but he watched with as much fascination as everyone else.

No one dared make a sound.

With a sudden move that startled everyone, Spock's hands jerked inwards and his fingers, still spread, started to shift backwards. They moved back, back, until the fingertips touched his head. The thumbs rested just under the earlobes and both little fingers met in a connecting line above the eyebrows.

The other fingers were fully extended and spread over his head, from forehead to just above the back hairline. He sat perfectly straight in the chair—rigid, motionless, even to the point of not appearing to breathe.

A voice spoke then ... but it didn't come from Spock. It had an eerie, faraway quality and emanated from a speaker in Uhura's console. The phenomenon was startling to hear. It was even more startling to see.

It was Spock ... and it wasn't.

"Listen To Me ... Listen to Me. You Are Not Alone Here. There is Someone Else. Listen To Me ... Listen To Me ... Listen to Me."

Seconds. Gone. Now.

Silence. The chronometer changing. Five to Four.

An explosion ... a tsunami of sound washed over them, swelling, to fill the bridge.

Uhura gave a little jump. Her free hand rushed reflexively to her earphone. She'd been prepared to detect, pick up the tiniest reply and had taken the full force of the aural jolt. It partially deafened her for a moment.

She adjusted a dial and brought the volume down. What came over the intricate farrago of circuitry and speakers was filtered via the slightly feminine alternate computer voice. It was hesitant ... only one word, but clear and recognizable ...

". . . WHAT . . . ?"

"You Are Not Alone Here," Spock repeated. "There is Someone Else. Listen To Me . . . Listen To Me . . . Listen To Me . . . .

Silence again. Then the voice that could only come from one place ... and every place. From all around them.

". . . WHAT . . . YOU . . . ?"

"I Am Another Being," said Spockvoice from the console.

It was like watching a shadow play. There was the silent, motionless figure of Spock, his lips unmoving and his voice speaking from a grid halfway across the room.

And another voice replying from out of nowhere. Spock repeated the words, again.

"I Am Another Being."

Vast immense slow voice.

"BEING . . . ? BEING . . . WHERE . . . ?"

"I Am Inside You."

"INSIDE . . . ? EXPLAIN. WITHIN ME . . . ?"

"I Am Very Small, And There Are Many of Me. We Are Within a Starship Which Is Within You."

". . . EXPLAIN . . . ELUCIDATE . . . CLARIFY . . ."

"A Small Thing That Holds All We Smaller Things. We Beings."

Somehow the great voice managed to sound astonished.

". . . THIS . . . WITHIN ME . . . ?"

"Within You."

And now, curious ...

". . . EXPLAIN . . . ?"

Kirk and McCoy exchanged desperate looks. At this rate it was going to be a long, complicated process ... too long.

The digital chronometer read 04.

"We Came To Think To You," Spock continued. "You Consumed Us. You Thought We Were Food."

". . . WHY . . . ? WHY YOU THINK TO . . . ME . . . ?"

Spock explained. "It Was Needed Done. Many of Us Live on Things You Consume."

". . . YOU LIVE ON THE THINGS I CONSUME . . . ?"

"Yes. Many of Us Live on One Such Thing Near You Now. Do Not Consume It."

". . . ELUCIDATE . . ."

"The Spherical Mass Ahead of You. The Matter You Intend to Ingest. Sense It Closely. Sense It . . . As You Sense Me. Do This Now . . . ."

There was a pause . . . they couldn't afford.

"How near is Mantilles now, Mr. Arex?" Kirk whispered.

"The cloud will impinge on the Mantillian atmosphere in three minutes, twenty seconds, sir."

"YES," came the voice finally. "I PERCEIVE MANY SOMETHINGS. SO . . . SMALL . . . !"

"They Are Still Beings," pressed Spock. "Alive . . . Like You. If You Consume Their Sphere-Thing-Home They Will All Die."

Another pause. Navigational controls all but forgotten, both Sulu and Arex stared fascinated at the chronometer. Their unwavering gaze failed to halt 04 from shifting down to 03. Sweating cold sweat, they looked back at Spock.

". . . TOO SMALL . . ."

"Explain," said Spock.

"I AM SMALL . . . SOMETHINGS I PERCEIVE . . . TOO SMALL. NOT ALIVE BEINGS . . . ."

Kirk hammered once, softly, on the arm of the command chair. There was no way, no way Spock could explain to it in time. How *could* he explain? How could a creature that dwarfed planets be convinced that there lived on those surfaces an intelligent mold called man?

"Listen To Me," Spockvoice murmured. "I Am Going To Come Into Your Mind. At The Same Time, You Must Come Into Mine. Do You Understand?"

". . . REASON(S) . . . ?"

"Then You Will Be Able To Sense What Kind of Beings We Are. You Will Sense We Are Alive."

". . . NECESSARY . . . ?"

Was there a hint of fear in that voice? Was the titanic, stellar-sized mass afraid?"

"Yes, Very," Spock insisted.

Yet another wait . . . longer, this time.

". . . PROCEED . . . ."

The first officer's hands reached out from his head again. His arms remained outstretched in front of him, fingers spread, palms upturned. No one breathed. No one moved. Several prayed.

Uhura forced herself to glance at her own console chronometer. Saw the 03 become 02. She stared at it, frozen, like a bird surprised by a snake.

Spock suddenly relaxed. He opened his eyes and looked around curiously—blank. Rising slowly from his seat he started to walk around the bridge.

He stared at Kirk, Dr. McCoy. At Arex and Sulu and Uhura, at the instruments on the console, the floor, the viewscreen, and then at his own hands and feet.

"Bones," Kirk whispered, realizing once more that in the vastness of the universe it was often the unspectacular that was truly awesome, "*he's the cloud*. Its thoughts are here."

Attracted by the sound of his voice, the Spock/cloud turned and walked over to him, stared, examined. As though using a strange new tool for the first time it put out a hand and touched Kirk's face. The hand moved awkwardly, roughly, and sensed what it touched.

McCoy made a move as if to interpose himself between Kirk and the Spock/cloud. Kirk's order was sharp.

"Don't move!"

Spock/cloud concluded its examination of Kirk and walked around the command chair. It looked curiously at the viewscreen, which still showed the diagram of the cloud's brain. Kirk kept his voice low as he spoke to Uhura.

"Lieutenant, use the library computer. Put some views of the Earth up there."

"Yes, sir." She moved cautiously to Spock's station, but it wasn't necessary. The Spock/cloud was thoroughly engrossed in the screen. Buttons were depressed, switches struck. The screen changed to a view of Earth taken from space. Kirk rose and stood next to Spock/cloud, talked to it smoothly.

"This is the thing we come from." He backed up a few steps, turned and whispered to Uhura.

"Lieutenant, this is what I want . . ."

The image on the screen changed, closing in on Earth until the continents—so familiar to Uhura, Sulu, and Kirk—showed. The picture moved in tighter on the Western Hemisphere, then on North America.

Uncaring of the frantic controlled activity going on around it, the chronometer adjusted from 02 to 01.

Still deeper moved the scene, for aerial views of cities. Closer and closer, as the timer began ticking off seconds.

People began to fill the screen . . . lots of people. People working, people playing, people eating and producing and reproducing and caring for children. Children playing as the chronometer went to thirty seconds.

"Awaiting your orders," said First Engineer Scott calmly. He stood waiting at the engineering console, his thumb over the flip-up protecting the double combination self-destruct lever. Kirk held up a warning hand.

"A few seconds yet, Scotty. We have to give Spock that much."

The pictures flashing on the screen concluded, fittingly—as Mantilles might—with children.

The chronometer said twenty seconds. Uhura wanted to scream.

She backed away from the library as the Spock/cloud turned slowly and walked back to its chair. It sat down easily and leaned back a little, slumped. Kirk returned quickly to his command seat.

McCoy's voice was husky. "Jim, it's got to be now. If we don't self-destruct now, all those people will be killed."

At McCoy's words, something suddenly died inside the captain. He felt amazingly calm, unafraid. And tired, so tired. *Just give the command, James, and you can rest. It'll be over in an instant—*

He turned to face Scott.

Like a man gasping his last breath while suddenly recalling his life, the chronometer went from 01 to 00 . . .

Sulu nearly leaped out of his seat.

"The cloud has stopped, Captain! The edge is just touching the outer atmosphere, but it has *stopped!*"

". . . COMPREHEND!" boomed the thunderous drone from Uhura's open speakers. ". . . NOT DESIRE TO CONSUME OTHER BEINGS . . ."

The cheering that erupted on the bridge was spontaneous and thoroughly undisciplined.

"Quiet!" Kirk shouted.

"There Are Many Things in Our Galaxy Like The One You Now Perceive," Spock continued, apparently unaffected by the outburst. He hadn't joined the cheering.

". . . TRUTH . . . ?" rumbled the voice.

"Truth. You Do Not Desire To Consume Other Beings. It Would Be Best Therefore If You Returned To Your Place of Origin The Way You Came. Will You Do This?"

". . . A LONG JOURNEY . . ."

"Will You Return?" The console Spockvoice was persistent—insistent.

Eventually the voice replied. Its tone was almost indifferent, as though its decision were of no consequence.

". . . PERCEIVE. WILL RETURN TO ORIGIN PLACE . . ."

There was a long wait. Then Arex spoke excitedly without shifting from his place at the helm.

"Sir, sensors indicate the cloud is moving *away* from Mantilles. And picking up speed rapidly!"

Kirk left his chair and moved quickly to Spock.

"Lieutenant Uhura, contact Governor Wesley and tell him he can bring his ships back. If he asks how and why, tell him it seems that armaggedon has a conscience."

"Yes, Captain!" Uhura's voice was alive with relief.

Kirk studied his first officer. He started to put a hand on Spock's shoulder. Maybe the slight touch—but it wasn't needed.

An exhausted Spock blinked his eyes, held them open, and looked up at Kirk.

"Spock, you did it! The cloud is leaving."

"I believe so, Captain. There is no way out from this sector. But there is a weblike arrangement of cloud-substance at the top of the brain. The cloud uses this thick grid to 'sense'—it is not exactly like sight—other things with. A combination eye, ear, and many other senses too alien, too strange, to attempt description." He shook his head, blinked again.

"I have had but the slightest touch with it . . . fortunately. Its intellectual potential is astounding, but it has developed in ways utterly different from anything previously imagined.

"This web at the top is dense by its own standards, yet comparatively empty by ours. We can escape through it." No time for idle questions here.

"Mr. Sulu! Let's get out of here. That grid's on the schematic . . . take us through."

Sulu's response was . . . well, agreeable. His hands played the helm like an organ. Kirk started back to his chair, paused at a sudden thought.

"Spock, while the cloud was here, in you, perceiving us, where were—" His eyes widened slightly. "You must have been in the *cloud*. What did *you* perceive?"

Spock's mind had returned to his body, but his thoughts were still elsewhere. He murmured softly.

"The wonders of the universe, Captain," he shook his head at the incredible memories.

Moments later they were free of the cloud, having encountered no trouble in passing between the moon-sized gaps in the cloud's sensing grid. Once back in free space, Kirk ordered the *Enterprise* in a tight circle that would bring her rapidly back to Mantilles. The starship could help supervise the return of the overcrowded evacuation ships.

But for the moment, his attention was focused on the screen. It showed the vast cloud-shape, now shrinking rapidly as it picked up speed, heading towards the outer fringes of the Milky Way. Spock was still staring after it, his mind filled with wonders he'd never be able to properly share with anyone else.

"Someday, Captain, when we are able to protect ourselves a little better, we may be fortunate enough to meet it again, or others like it."

"And when that day comes," Kirk agreed softly, caught up in Spock's own sense of wonder—and his own emotional release—"when that day comes, Mr. Spock, the ant will stand on its hind legs and converse with the man . . ."

Together they stayed watching the screen until the last faint hint of cloud was gone.

Only infinity and a few stars remained.